LOST AT THE CON

This one is for the geeks, the girls,

and Anakin and Scout.

-BY 2011

LOST AT THE CON

Part One: Assignment

I

"Cobb, get in here."

It was these four simple words that shattered my weekend, and probably the rest of my life, into a million tiny razor blades.

The voice that spoke these terrible words belonged to my editor. My editor was an overweight Gila monster of a man with wide set eyes and thin, cracking lips to match. He poured sweat and shouted like a yappy dog, constantly out of breath. How he'd risen to the rank of editor was anyone's guess. I thought he was a prick when he offered me a steady check and my opinion of him hasn't improved in the last twenty-eight months. I wanted to go back to freelance, but it was too tough, so here I am with a steady check and not a shred of self respect left to my name. I was hoping to find some around any corner, but with this gig I doubted it.

Bryan Young

The gig was writing for a few online rags, but mainly one called *Titan*, which was a second rate caricature of *Maxim*, which was itself a second rate caricature of the shit *Playboy* had turned into. Thanks to *US Weekly* and Perez Hilton, we were all whores now, circling the drain, faster and faster.

"I got something for you," he told me after I sat down in his untidy sanctuary. I had a hard time looking at the wheezy bastard so I always wore dark sunglasses in his office. That always pissed him off, but I didn't care. I could stare at the wall while he barked like an underweight Chihuahua. I'm sure it made him twice as mad to see my gaunt face framing his revolting reflection.

"Oh yeah?"

"It's hot."

"Is it anything like last time?"

"No. Forget about last time. Last time was a clusterfuck. This time I've got a thing we've never covered before. You know how much all that geek shit gets a shitload a eyeballs on the page, and I think it suits you. I'm sending you to Griffin*Con. It's down in Atlanta."

Yap, yap, yap.

"Send someone else."

"There is no one else. And I think you'll have a fresh take on the whole thing. It'll get you out a your comfort zone. You've been on auto-pilot lately."

"If we've never covered it before, anybody can make it fresh. What about Jones? He's into all that geek shit."

I was staring at the papers on his desk hoping to find interesting reading material I could peruse from my vantage point during this defecation of a conversation.

"He'd write it up just like everybody else who's going. He's too close to all that stuff. It doesn't matter though. I sent him to the city. He's taking care of a string of wet T-shirt contests." This is what passes for journalism. "Besides, the ticket's already booked in your name."

Fuck it. I tell myself over and over there's a paycheck to be had whether the stories I turn in are any good or not. And, let's be honest, what passes for "good" in this place isn't exactly Pulitzer material. "You can't just make me go at the snap of your fingers."

"The hell I can't. You signed an employment contract. You go if the story's hot, day or night, near or far, in a house with a mouse, in a box with a fox. And I say this story is hot."

I must have been drunk when I signed that damn thing. It didn't matter. I guess a weekend out of this festering bog couldn't be all that bad. Maybe I'd find that self-respect I was searching high and low for. "Jesus Christ, when is this thing?"

"You leave in the morning. It starts on Friday, the day after. You'll be on a plane back Sunday night."

"That's *this* weekend?" The bastard. I've been given less notice on big stories before, that's just the way journalism works, especially in Washington, but this son of a bitch just handed me a four day assignment, a thousand miles away and through my weekend, on twelve hours notice.

I vowed that I would spend the rest of the meeting imagining that I was cutting out his filthy, little heart with a dull and dirty knife.

"I'm gonna need at least half a dozen good stories out a this from you. Maybe more. Otherwise it isn't worth our dime."

"Half a dozen? Can't I just write a cover story?"

"Cover of what? The demographic advertising needs us to hit doesn't read anything over 350 words."

"I don't have time for brevity if I'm doing a series on shit I know nothing about."

"Not my problem. I want at least one story a night filed while you're gone. I don't care what they're about, but this stuff is big in certain circles. Anything you write up'll get read. There's panels, costumes, all that kinda stuff."

"What kind of editor are you? You're hanging me out to dry. This is bullshit."

"You'll do fine." Smugly, he tossed my itinerary across the desk at me. At just a glance I could see on the printouts that he'd made the reservations in my name a couple of months ago. I pointed at the date on the paper, "What the hell is this?"

"Must have slipped my mind."

In my brain, his chest was simply a gaping hole of raw hamburger and spurting blood. His heart was in my hand and I could see myself taking a bite out of it if I thought for a moment his spirit had anything worth absorbing. Instead, I stuck the knife in his heart and tossed both over my shoulder. For some reason, I had his necktie tied around my melon like a headband cutting into my thick black hair and my sleeves were cut and frayed at the edges. Below my thin, doughy waist, I was wearing what could only be described as a barbarian's furry diaper. My legs were white and pale, and my feet were sandaled in leather straps.

I jumped down off of his desk and ran as fast as my ema-ciated frame could take me all the way to the too-small apartment I shared with my sometimes girlfriend. Just thinking about her angelic face was enough to make me smile. She was beautiful and, as clichéd as it sounded, I fell in love with her the moment I met her. It was at an art gallery and she was sitting on a bench, sketching the broad strokes of Maynard Dixon's "No Place To Go" into her little book. The first thing I ever noticed about her was that she had the most amazing hands. One of my favorite things in the world was to watch her brush her long, thick, mane of hair. It was like she was conducting an orchestra, her hands moved with such grace and care.

When I arrived home, I was left the unenviable task of telling her I had to leave town in the morning.

"I don't care."

"Oh."

"Why would I care?"

Our relationship was complicated, to say the least.

"I don't know. If the shoe were on the other foot I'd be a little annoyed with your employer."

"You're the asshole who decided to work for him. You got what you deserve."

"That's a pretty bleak way of looking at it."

"So? It's fine. I was planning on having people over anyway."

"Who? What people?"

"Not your problem."

"Seriously, who is it?"

"Some people I met. Don't worry about it. You'll be gone. If you were here, they'd only interrupt your bender anyway."

"Jesus. It's not a bender. I just think my prose is better when I drink."

"Tell yourself that. You haven't written any prose in a year. And you hate it when I bring guys over."

Fuck. That was the last straw. I needed a drink or I was going to collapse from the depression. I couldn't think of anything more heartbreaking than not having anyone in my life I could rely on. No one had my back. I had no idea what love was and monogamy was something I needed, but I had no clue how to find it. Hell, maybe I didn't love Laurie. And maybe it was just the communist in me that kept her around to share expenses. I don't know.

I was at least sentimental enough to never hurt her by bringing other guys home. Or, I mean, women. Fuck. You know what I mean. I don't like seeing her sleep with other men is what I'm saying. Despite my frequent drunkenness, I'm a pretty sensitive soul. And whether we're technically together at any given moment or not, we still live together.

It just hurts my feelings.

I wanted to be with her, even if she had turned into the Wicked Witch of the West. I wanted to have her respect. Maybe that was the problem, that it was a matter of respect. When we met I was a much happier person, but this job had sucked the life and enthusiasm out of me. She used to sit and watch me type and read pieces of my dystopian epic over my shoulder. She only watched me type prose. She used to say when I was working on a story for *Titan* my face grew hard and it was painful to watch.

She used to love falling asleep to the sound of me typing. In fact, she bought me an old automatic Corona typewriter to use for my rough drafts because she knew how much I liked the feel of a type-writer for my prose and the sound of it was soothing to her.

I hadn't plugged it in since I took this job.

Fuck.

I loved her. And I hadn't had the courage to tell her how much she meant to me.

Could you love me if you were her?

I couldn't either. Not with me being like I am. Now you see why I drink.

"Scotch."

"You got it, Cobb."

Scotty slammed a shot glass down on the bar in front of me, loaded it up, and I slammed it down my gullet.

"Tonight's my last night here for a while, Scotty."

"We'll miss you."

Somehow, I doubted it. Those were the last words he said to me all night that didn't have anything to do with collecting money for the string of drinks I'd ordered.

Since no one was talking to me and since no one seemed to want to listen to me anyway, I pulled out my notebook and pen and scratched out the rest of a piece I'd been working on about the House Majority Leader's absurd tan. Politics was my regular beat and insulting stupid-looking politicians was about as close to the TMZ trash-writing as I care to get. But like I said, it's a paycheck.

At some point I'd have to go back home, pack for my journey, type up and email the tan story, and who knows what else. And I'd have to do all of that through the fog of the drunken stupor I'd thrust myself into.

Jesus Christ.

I don't remember much of what happened in those next few hours, but I did manage to pull off a minor miracle and somehow cross all of those items off my "fuck-or-walk" list.

I'm sure I under packed, but I couldn't really get any smellier than a convention center full of geeks anyway, right? And I'm sure I could find some clothes to buy out there if I needed them. It's not like they don't sell textiles in Atlanta. Besides, I was already overburdened with extra bags for the tools of my trade: a computer, notebooks, pens, pencils, style-guides, a dictionary, and a thesaurus.

I would have liked to bring a cell-phone, but mine was broken and I didn't care enough to replace it yet. And, with my luck, a cell-phone would just give me brain cancer.

Some time, a couple of hours before the car would arrive to pick me up, I fell asleep. In slumber-land, I dreamt of many things. The image that stuck out the most during my throbbing hangover the next morning was one of me in a gang. I had an Uzi and an AK-47 and I was dressed in a wife-beater and a do-rag. I remember leaving my mother's house in that ridiculous get-up, crying, knowing that death was imminent. I knelt down on the way out, in front of a little brother I never had, chiding him to not take up the life I'd led. Laurie was, of course, shouting in the background to get out and so I left, gats in each hand, ready to meet my destiny.

The company car arrived with the sunrise. Its bleating horn aroused me from my gangsta dreams and I stood, scratching myself.

After blinking a few times and trying to find the will to live, I said, "Screw it," to no one in particular and collected my bag. I washed the awful taste in my mouth out with a shot of cheap, store-brand mouthwash I kept in the medicine cabinet, and then a shot of whiskey from an equally plastic bottle I kept beside the mouthwash.

I made it out to the garbage strewn street, bleary-eyed and still drunk, my hands full of bags. The company car was waiting for me there. It was an old Lincoln Town Car that had been faded gray with a thick membrane of dust and grime. It wasn't actually owned by the company, but they had retained this second-rate car service because somehow, in the final accounting, it was cheaper than the cab tab they had been paying for. My educated guess was that the owner of the car service was blowing the editor.

I waited for the driver to get out, open the trunk, and help me with my bags. Instead, the trunk popped open on its own, leaving me to stuff the bags in myself right next to the muddy, flat spare tire.

Once everything was in, I slammed the trunk closed and got in the back seat. "Airport, right?"

I grumbled in the affirmative and limply waved my hand at him in the general direction of the airport.

I closed my eyes hoping to go to sleep, but that's when the smell of stale farts, day old sex, and cardamom hit me in the face with both barrels. I almost lost the booze and bile in my gullet, but I caught it in my throat and choked it back down before I added a whole new array of unwanted liquids and aromas to the upholstery.

It was so bad that I spent the entire drive gulping breath through my mouth and holding it in as long as I could, the same way you would when you're in a bathroom that permeates fecal potpourri.

Since the noxious aroma that began as molecules festering in some filthy asshole were so bad, there was no way I could get back to sleep. To distract myself, I daydreamed about what this convention would most assuredly be like. The image I conjured was a sea of middle-aged, sexless eunuchs; each of them clutching a purse full of dice in one hand and a stack of thick roleplaying books in the other. Often when I don't know about something, I think about it in the most basic stereotypes I could imagine. Sure, my expectations would probably be challenged, but it just goes to show you how little I know about all this stuff. In high school, I was too busy working on my school newspaper and writing fiery editorials about the administration to pay much attention to the nerds. Same with the jocks. I couldn't stand any of them. They all seemed so damned useless to me.

I did have more in common with the nerds, though. If I were stuck dealing with the nerds, there were certainly things we could talk about. I read comic books in school, watched science fiction movies, the whole nine yards. I just didn't wear it on my sleeve like those guys. And I left it all in behind me in high school.

Kids games.

I must admit some part of me still wants to write a science fiction novel, something that would make Rod Serling smile.

As soon as we rolled up to the airport I leapt out of the car, escaping the ass-molecules as quickly as I could. The driver made no move to help me with my bags again, so as a tip I threw a handful of hard change at him through the passenger window and ran away, fearing retaliation.

I'm kind of a wuss like that.

The security rituals at the airport were absurd and needlessly invasive. They needed to X-ray everything: my computer, my phone, my bag, my belt, my shoes, what was left of my change, my wallet. I even had to toss out a bottle of water. It seemed to me that it was a racket perpetrated by suppliers of bottled water inside the secured areas of the airport. Sure, it was gin in my bottle, but they didn't know that. Besides, whoever heard of a plane being hijacked by a bottle of water? It just screams industry scam.

I got two books of matches through, though. Light it up. No problem.

Maybe I'd write a piece about that and try to sell it to *Newsweek* or something. Maybe I'd frame it around the idea that lightning never strikes the same place twice and how we're not promoting safety with all these extra precautions, merely the illusion of it.

It could be good. Or not. I really wouldn't know until someone bought it or didn't.

Between the car service, Checkpoint Charlie style security screening, and my pending trip to Nerdland, my patience was wearing thin. By the time I got to my boarding gate, I was ready to get on and hijack the plane myself. I'd have them land it on a desert island where I could frolic in the sand and work on my book, completely cut off from the outside world.

I'd drink coconuts and eat fish.

The other survivors would thank me for it.

I'm glad I stopped to close my eyes and take a breath to calm down before I got on the plane to Atlanta, because I discovered quickly that I was seated between a mother with a screaming child on one side, and an unaccompanied minor on the other.

There went any chance of a peaceful flight.

"Stewardess?" I shouted after the well-dressed and obviously male flight attendant. "I need a drink."

"You'll have to wait until the plane is in the air, sir." His face suppressed a laugh when he saw the kids on either side of me, an obvious drunk with no patience and no coping skills. This bastard understood my thirsty desires and saw fit to just walk away in my hour of need.

I unfolded the newspaper I'd tucked under my arm at some point that I had no recollection of purchasing. I wanted to read it, but was interrupted by a tap on my shoulder. As I turned to give this little unaccompanied bastard what for, I realized that it was the male stewardess, drink in hand.

With a lisp and a wink, "You seem like a scotch on the rocks sort of guy."

Maybe he wasn't so bad after all.

I gulped the scotch down as quickly as possible and spent the long torturous hours on the flight distracting myself with the Washington Post's crossword puzzle. The whole thing wasn't so bad, but I still fled the plane as soon as I could, like a lone, sane man fleeing a room full of flesh-eating zombies.

I collected my bags without incident and boarded the mass-transit train that would take me into Atlanta. If my itinerary was to be trusted, the train would let me off just two blocks from my hotel. It was a bit of work, trying to figure out how to buy a transit ticket and get onto the right train, but I just followed the group of overweight mouth-breathers in self-made "Griffin*Con or Bust" T-shirts.

These guys made me feel like my worst fears about this whole weekend were going to be realized.

I hopped aboard the same train as they did, hoping we'd be getting off at the same stop so I could follow them to the hotel without incident. Finding a seat behind them at the back of the train, I settled in and watched them, hoping I could find a story to turn in.

There were three of them. One was male, early thirties with long black hair and a patchy beard that must have taken him weeks to grow. The next was a woman with a bad complexion and a mane of frazzled red hair. Her glasses must have been ground from a two-inch sheet of glass or an actual Coke bottle. The sex of the third could not be determined. It was dressed in the same uniform as the other two, was clean-shaven with a bad complexion, and had a shoulder-length mound of curly black hair. Its voice was no better indication, for all intents and purposes it was completely androgynous and it caused a shiver of confused fear and disgust to run up my back.

Their discussion seemed to revolve around some sort of game.

The male of this foreign species was going on about some stunning defeat he'd had at the hands of some mythical creature or another. "I still can't believe I critical follied my roll to lance the beast. It was, perhaps, the most humiliated I've been in a long time."

The androgynous one responded, "And what did the folly chart come up with for you?"

"My lance hit the ground and pole-vaulted me into the beast. I took so much damage, I won't even begin to tell you."

The one I assumed was female chimed in finally, "It was the funniest thing I'd ever seen. The GM couldn't get through reading the folly result without laughing and Bill spit out half his beer on the floor."

"That's funny", it said, with no hint of laughter or joy. Not only was it devoid of sex, it was also completely humorless, too.

I groaned.

If this was what I had to look forward to for the rest of the trip, I might go out like the Texas Tower Sniper. Which would be a remarkable thing, since I abhor guns and wouldn't even know where to find one. But somehow, listening to these people, I could very easily see myself ending their lives from the top of a tower at three klicks.

I'm not a socio-path, I swear. I just have a pretty violent and easily annoyed imagination. At least that's what I've been telling myself all these years. I'm too passive aggressive to actually hurt anybody. I'll keep telling myself that for as long as I find myself not actually hurting anyone. Until I do hurt somebody, I'm clearly not capable of hurting anyone.

Seriously.

I'm pretty sure I'm not going to hurt anyone.

But these self-importance filled knuckle draggers were going to push me right over the edge. I'll admit, they didn't deserve to die, to each their own, but they kept going on in the most inane ways. The man kept rolling an imaginary pair dice in front of himself to the point where I couldn't tell if he was trying to shoot craps or pretending to jerk off onto his she-male friend.

I tried to block them out and drink in the view of the Atlanta skyline as we approached it by rail. It didn't take long for me to determine that I couldn't tell it apart from any other mid-sized metropolises I'd been to in the line of duty. I doubt I would have ever visited Atlanta if I hadn't been sent there. In fact, without any specific reason whatsoever, I found myself wishing Sherman hadn't just burned Atlanta to the ground, but had in fact salted it completely.

There goes my imagination again.

The skyline and above-ground rails gave way to darkness and under-ground subway lines. It wasn't more than a couple of stops before it was time to get off. I followed my nerdy canaries into the coal mine of the Atlanta underground, but I lost them in the masses. There was only one direction to go and it led to an escalator that seemed two miles long. It boggled my mind how it not only held as much weight as it did at capacity, but that it conveyed it upwards and onwards out onto the city streets of Atlanta.

I hit the pavement and confusion bathed me in a cold sweat. Towering over me in every direction were high rises. I was beneath a canopy, so I couldn't see the sky, but it seemed to be a cool, gray autumn morning. My overweight and erstwhile guideposts had blended in so well with the street crowd that I had no idea which direction to turn.

"Hey, man."

I could see no reason why this voice would be calling out to me, but apparently it was.

"What hotel you looking for?"

"Huh?" I looked around, trying to identify the voice.

"Which hotel you tryin' to get to?" I finally spotted the man talking, a lanky black man in a T-shirt two sizes too big. It was frayed at the edges and had a logo for something I didn't recognize faded on the front.

"Uhh..." I was instantly wary of him. Not because he was black, but because he was obviously from Atlanta.

"You here for the 'Con, right?"

"Yeah."

"Shit, man. I could tell just by looking at ya."

"Really?"

"Hell yeah. Nobody comes to this part a town durin' the 'Con with any sort a luggage unless they goin'. So which hotel you at?"

"The Marriott Marquis."

"Come on, the hotel's this way."

Without a second for me to think better of this, I followed this strange Atlantean (they're Atlantean's right?) around the corner and down a shady looking street. But to be fair, with my apparent and unfounded dislike of Atlanta, all of the streets seemed shady, like a knife would find purchase in my back at any moment.

"Shit, man, the look on your face, I thought you were stayin' at some place way out of town, but your place is close, man."

"Oh, yeah?"

"Yeah, man. You looked like a kid away from home. So you ready to party?"

We turned a corner and waited to cross a street.

"Ummm..." I was simply bewildered by the friendly nature of this person. My only conclusion could be that he wasn't actually from Atlanta, but some place out west and was trapped here in this stinking hell-hole. Why else would you be in the south? What with the systemic racism and that time they tried to tear the country in half? Fuck those guys.

"You ever been to a con, man?"

"No. This is my first one."

"Shit, man. This place is a par-tay. You guys for this shit really know how to party, like, it doesn't stop, man."

"Are you here for the con?"

"No, man. I'm homeless. I work the conventions now and again setting stuff up, but mostly I'm just homeless."

"Oh."

"This place is always better when the Con is goin' on, though."

"It certainly couldn't get any worse."

"This place ain't so bad."

"If you say so."

We reached another intersection and the homeless man pointed down the street to the right. "Down that way, that's where the party is all the time. That restaurant, it don't close. There's a party going on there from tonight through the weekend, it's fuckin' kickin'."

He pointed down the left, "Now we're gonna cross down this street, and then your hotel is gonna be right here close. C'mon."

The light changed and we crossed the street. I had to readjust the bag over my shoulder, I almost lost my grip on it. If I dropped it I didn't know how long I'd have before some Atlantean street vulture snatched it from me.

"So, man. This is it. This is you right here, man. You just head up that walkway there and you at the Marriott lobby. It'll be a party in there all weekend, too, for sure."

Despite my general distrust of strangers, I was thankful for this homeless man's help. I'd have been walking the streets for hours looking for the hotel, giving myself an ulcer in the process. Or I'd have taken a cab. One way or the other.

"Thanks for the help."

"No sweat, man. But now that I helped you, you think you can help me out, like help me get something to eat tonight?"

Normally, I'd be pretty pissed about this, but he seemed like a nice guy and I was going to expense this as a cab ride anyway. I placed a pair of my bags at my feet, clenching them between my legs so no one could steal them and fished out my wallet. I had a wide array of bills in my wallet, including a few singles, but I opted for one of the larger bills. I pulled out a twenty and handed it to him.

"For reals?"

"I'm not using it."

Full of thanks, he snatched the bill and offered his hand for a shake. "Shit, man. You're all right. My name's Sylvester."

Warily, I shook his hand. "Cobb."

"Cobb, you should come on down and hang out tonight, man. You're all right."

"Maybe. I don't know what's going on. You'll be out here?"

"Yeah, man. I got no where else to be."

We shook hands again and he left with a smile on his face. I can't imagine being homeless and happy. I'm not really sure who the hell I am to judge, though. I'm well sheltered and miserable. I bet he's happy because he doesn't have a girl like Laurie to come home to. And I bet his non-Laurie doesn't bring home guys to fuck. Or at least wouldn't if they had a home to go to.

Each step I took into the hotel lobby was pregnant with jealousy. The only images my mind could conjure were those of Laurie bringing home guys by the pair. It was disgusting.

I had less than no interest in dealing with the concierge.

"What's the name on the reservation, sir?"

Without saying a word I handed him the itinerary my editor had given me, which was what I thought to be a clear indication that I had no desire to speak to him whatsoever. Despite my expectations and deepest wishes, he kept talking to me. I responded the entire time in grunts, completely non-verbally. He waved piece of paper after piece of paper in my face, asking for signatures and initials. I finished it all, signing everything "Adolf Hitler" and filling out each space for initials "FU". Sure it was juvenile, but I was going to have to get some enjoyment out of this trip, even if it was just to giggle about it to myself later in the hotel room.

He finally handed me the keycard to my room.

"Room 903."

"Blah."

"Enjoy your stay, sir."

"Fuck off."

I walked away and got my first real look at the Marriott Marquis Atlanta. It was massive, rising thirty or forty stories up, but the center of the building was a lobby and bar on the main floor and open air all the way up to the top. Every floor had a completely encircling balcony that overlooked the lobby and in the center was an elevator system that went all the way to the top and all points in between.

At the base of the elevators were cool blue fountains that dozens of poor saps had dropped hundreds of pennies into the bottom of. It made me wish I was foolish enough to drop a wish into a fountain.

You know what I'd wish for? Laurie. And the courage to finish my novel. A novel about something important. Maybe even a little science-fictiony, Ray Bradbury style. Real literary sci-fi, not the kind I bet was popular with the dregs around here.

But I didn't see that happening any time soon.

The hotel décor was earth toned, browns and beiges set against deep red carpets. Sure it was crass, but the color scheme reminded me of the phrase "Mediterranean menstruation." The legs were the beige balconies crawling all the way up to the sky, bleeding out all over the floor. Gross? Yes. But like I said, I had to entertain myself somehow.

The elevators were made of plexi-glass panels that were glued together into a cylindrical shape so someone could look out over the whole of the stately Marriott courtyard during their ascent. The molding and fixtures of the elevator were made of cheap brass and it was carpeted in the same brownish-red flooring. I pushed the button.

Ninth floor, here I come.

The lift was so fast I thought I might vomit, spilling the precious alcohol from my system. This would not do, not do at all. As soon as I dropped my bags off, my first order of business was to find a drink and get my press credentials. After that, priority numero uno would be to get to the bottom of what this whole thing was about. As far as I knew, geeks were all thirty-something acne farms, living in their parents' basement and pontificating about the differences between versions of *Star Wars* movies and an encyclopedic knowledge of cultures in *Star Trek* I'd never hope to be able to pronounce. But there was something about a gathering of this nature that didn't jive with that stereotype. The sort of person who put themselves out there in so public a situation wasn't a basement dwelling mouth-breather.

Maybe it could be an interesting piece for me to work on. Scratching the surface beneath the psyche of these bottom feeders. You look at all the biggest movies, the bestselling books, the richest people in the world, and the popular culture in general and it's pretty easy to see that the geeks have inherited the Earth. But why?

The more I thought about this assignment the more I hated it. I just wanted to go home and write something worthwhile. If ever I wanted to do that I'd have to get through this bullshit assignment and I was going to have to file at least a pair of stories tonight.

Shit.

"Jack and a Coke."

I drank down my refreshing, intoxicating beverage and paid the man behind the hotel bar. The alcohol in it wasn't enough to bring me into drunkenness but it certainly bit back at the hangover from before. Drunkenness would come later.

With any luck, not much later.

Consulting the notes I made in my drunken stupor the night before, I knew that my press credentials could be picked up on the bottom floor of the Hyatt Regency hotel in the media headquarters, which I was informed by another passing hobo, was just across the street from the Marriott. The hobos were ubiquitous. They seemed to know the ins and outs of the convention, too, which led me to surmise that they were something like urban longshoremen. The force that put the facilities together for the convention must have been entirely made up of the homeless of Atlanta.

I jaywalked across the street, up a steep staircase and was, sure enough, brought to the back of a hotel through a massive glass door. There were meeting rooms to my left and a maze of escalators running every which way to my right. In the center was a small white booth that reminded me of the psychiatry lemonade stand from Peanuts. The only difference was that "Griffin*Con Information" was written along the top instead of "The Doctor is: IN".

"Excuse me. Where's the media room?"

There was a fellow behind the information counter with an earpiece connected to a walkie-talkie poring over notebooks and maps of the convention. If he had some dice I would have assumed him to be role-playing with himself.

"Media room?"

"Yeah."

"Do you guys know where the media room is?"

"That's what I'm asking you."

He shushed me and pointed to his earpiece. He enunciated once more, this time in an even more obnoxious and clueless tone, "Media room. Yeah. Where?"

Someone was clearly talking back to him, his eyes were glazed over, listening hard, and his head bobbed back and forth like a curious bird. Finally, he pulled the earpiece out and directed his attention back to me. "It's down this escalator, past the comics hall, down that escalator, make two rights and it'll be straight ahead to your right."

"Uh..."

"Down the escalator, past the comics hall, down that escalator, two rights, straight ahead to the right. Got it?"

I walked away, confident I'd find it somehow. By the way this idiot was talking, I'd need a map, a GPS, and a compass before I'd be likely to find it. It wasn't hard to figure out the first part: going down the escalator behind him and finding another one somewhere else to head down. What the hell, I'd start with that and see where it led me.

Predictably, it led me down to the next level, which looked exactly like the level above. It was a maze of meeting rooms, escalators and whatnot. This level had the added bonus of being host to a series of tables set up along the perimeter against the wall. The signs and banners pinned above and below the tables identified them as the headquarters for various fan-based organizations that I'd never hope to understand.

"Join the Browncoats!"

"Mandalorian Mercs: We always get our man."

"The 501st Legion wants YOU to join the Empire"

"Carolina Ghostbusters. We're ready to believe you!"

"Colonial Space Marines"

And on and on and on. The lobby area these tables occupied was deserted except for passersby. I was curious to see what the people filling this space up in the coming days would look like. Only time would tell.

There was a break in the tables in the back corner of the lobby area for three huge sets of wood-paneled doors. In front of them was an easel with a massive sign on it that informed all comers that the comics hall lay behind. I was on the right path, though I didn't see any fucking escalator. Did he say it was in the Comics Hall? Or behind it? Somewhere in this vicinity?

Nothing ventured, nothing gained. I ducked my head into the center set of chestnut doors, saw that no one was around to stop me and walked into the Comics Hall. Again, it wasn't set up in any meaningful way. I'd been to enough conventions of various types to know how a room like this was supposed to look, and I could imagine what it would look like when all of the exhibitors were in place and completely set up, but until then it was a ghost town of banners and tables. There were a few exhibitors, presumably writers or artists in the comics field, setting up their wares for sale in this miniature version of an exhibition hall.

I took a walk around inside to see what there was to see. The thing that caught my eye almost immediately was a vinyl banner across the hall with a scantily clad and impossibly out of proportion Amazon on it. On a similar banner to its right was a beautiful woman with striking eyes that could have passed for

Wonder Woman holding a dachshund. For reasons I couldn't fathom, there was a screaming monkey brandishing a knife pictured between them. Booth after booth featured illustrators and their creations that were recognizable figures from my youth, guys like Superman or Spider-Man. Some looked amateurish, but most of the banners were slick and sexy. If these were what comics looked like these days, they'd changed a lot since my day. Back then, comics were wordy, cheap newsprint that served as something barely worth reading. This stuff was actually impressive. And that rendition of a hot green chick labeled She-Hulk on the other side of the room was dangerously close to giving me an actual erection.

There was a fellow at one of the tables unloading books from a plastic tub, readying them for sale and display. He was rotund, had a thick, well-groomed Vandyke the same length as his hair, and he wore the sort of button up shirt you'd imagine seeing a middle-aged businessman wear on vacation in 1955. If the signage at his table was to be believed, he wrote and drew some sort of comic book about a mook or a hooligan or something. "You know which direction to the media room? They told me it was past the comics hall and down the next escalator, but this place is a fucking maze."

"Umm... I think the only down escalators near here are behind the ones just outside."

"No shit?"

"Yeah."

"So, uh, when does this whole thing start?"

"Tomorrow, officially. Everything's still being set up."

"And you're going to be here all weekend, selling your funny books?"

"Something like that."

"I'm a reporter."

"Cool."

"I'm not sure why I'm covering this thing, politics is my beat. This is all a foreign language to me."

"I bet."

This guy couldn't be less impressed with me and my blathering small talk. I really am an idiot.

"You do these often?"

"Maybe ten a year."

"They worth it for you? Coming to these I mean?"

"Totally. I make a killing with sketches and signing books."

"Sketches?"

"Yeah. I charge fifty bucks a pop for a sketch of whatever people want. They take me twenty minutes. Ten of those in a day and I'm up five hundred bucks. Other guys do lots more than that, though. Archie," he pointed to a booth across the room with some noir-ish looking superhero girls adorning it, "he charges two-fifty a sketch and only does five a day. I've heard of him walking out of a con with ten-grand from sketches."

"People pay that?"

"Sure."

"Hmm. Well, I'll let you go. I've got to find my credentials."

"Sure thing."

"Nice talking to you."

"Likewise."

I left the way I came and sure enough, there was an escalator heading down right behind the escalators I'd come down in the first place. I was going to have to work on my internal compass if I was going to get around this place. No matter what direction I went, I felt completely turned around and disoriented.

It took forty-five minutes of trial and error, traversing through the webbed network of hallways and meeting rooms in the Hyatt, to finally make my way into the media room. I always expect some sort of hi-tech war room for the media room, monitors and super-computers everywhere, cables crisscrossing the walls, rotary phones at every workstation for calling in reports. Behind a desk I'd like to see a throwback from a William Gibson novel with an Internet cable jacked directly into his asshole for some reason. My version would have been more glamorous, but this dump looked like any other cheap meeting room at a hotel. On the far side of the room was a pudgy bearded man sitting behind a milk-crate full of manila envelopes and a laptop borne out of the early nineties. A table full of cheap coffee and bagels, presumably for the press, occupied the other side of the room. White table-clothes covered every surface and the mood was solemn, giving off the impression that this was either a cheap wedding or a fancy AA meeting.

Expectantly, the bearded man waited for me to come over, but I helped myself to a bagel and two cups of coffee first, my back turned to him the entire time. Though I couldn't see the look on his face, I imagine he kept that same nervous smile on it throughout, trying to ease the tension building inside of him, watching me eat and slurp coffee slowly from behind.

Gin would have been a better option, but apparently they weren't interested in keeping the working press happy. Also, it was barely noon.

The man behind the counter coughed, hoping to get my attention. It worked.

"What outlet are you covering this for?" The voice coming out of the hole in his salt and pepper facial hair was meek with a touch of femininity.

"*Titan.*"

He repeated that word over and over again, rolling it up and down his tongue as he flipped through each and every sealed envelope in his milk crate until he came to the right one. "Mr. Cobb?"

I held out my hand and coughed dryly.

"Here you are, sir. Let me know if there's anything else I can help you with."

The envelope was thick and I tore it open, hoping the entire time that it was secret instructions for a mission for Her Majesty's Secret Service. Hell, I'd have settled for the CIA. To my eternal disappointment, it was a two-hundred page guide to the convention and an overly ornate name badge with a griffin swooping and screeching and who knows what else on the front. The stiff, amateur artwork was covered over at the bottom by a white shipping label with my name spelled wrong in smeared inkjet ink. They had me down as Cob with one "b", not realizing that only a jackass would have only one "b". Dangling beneath my misspelled name was a day-glo orange ribbon with the word "Press" emblazoned on it white lettering.

They may as well have painted a target on my forehead.

"So, where's the convention center?"

"You're in the convention center."

"I'm in a hotel."

"The main convention actually takes place in four hotels. There's a mall and a skywalk connecting this one to the Marriott, and then there's a skywalk connecting the Marriott to the Hilton. The Sheraton is a couple of blocks away and it houses the Yule Ball and other social events and a few panels. There's a map in your events guide."

"Sounds like I'll need it."

"If you need any help for interview requests or stories, let me know, and we'll accommodate you as best we can. I have a phone list of all the publicists for the celebrities, so I can help you out if you need interviews."

"Anybody famous here?"

"Anybody famous? Why don't you look through your guide and get back to me and let me know if there's anyone famous here. Or better yet, why don't you take a walk through the autograph hall. If there's anybody there you want to talk to, let us know, we'll do our best to make it happen. And we hope to see you at the press welcome party tonight."

My ears perked up.

"Press welcome party?"

"Yes. It starts at seven and it'll be in suite 2420 at the Marriott."

I patted my pockets looking for my notebook to write that down in. That was the first important piece of information I'd been privy to all week. Seeing my struggle, the awkward little man wrote the room number and hotel down on a post-it note and handed it to me.

"You'll be able to meet some of the other press and some of the celebrities will be showing up."

I grunted my thanks and left, greedily clutching the post-it note. I was confident that if I didn't see him at the press party, I'd never see him again.

It was another two hours of wandering before I finally made it to my hotel room and took a much-needed nap.

THE STARTLING ECONOMICS OF GRIFFIN*CON
by M. Cobb

ATLANTA, GA -- Atlanta hosts what might be the
most popular party convention for science fiction
geeks in the world. Griffin*Con has been described as the "Mardis Gras of Comic-Conventions"
and "a three day geek bender", but there's a seedy
underbelly to the merriment not outwardly apparent
to the average convention-goer. From price gouging to preying on the homeless, the geeks in
charge seem to know no shame in their quest to
throw their party.

Sylvester Catman is a 35 year-old African American
male and one of Atlanta's homeless. He is dirty
and disheveled, reeks of week-old body odor, but
has a likable air to him. He roams the streets by
day and night and makes ends meet by working as
some kind of modern day longshoreman, assembling
booths and tables to provide the infrastructure
for Griffin*Con. "I suppose it's better than
nothing, but not much. I've got to eat and this
is the only job I can find. Pays less than minimum wage, but it's all under the table, so I don't
need an address or nothing."

On the outside of the exhibition hall, Sylvester
was panhandling, hoping to make ends meet for his
family. On the inside, comic book artists were
making a killing. One comic artist found hocking
his wares who spoke under the condition of anonym-
ity said, "I'll make $5,000, maybe $6,000 this
weekend, selling books and doing sketches. It's

not unheard of for some of these guys to charge a
few hundred dollars a sketch. One artist here
left his last convention with almost $20,000 in
his pocket."

And so it is always with the excesses of the popular culture and entertainment, exploiting an infrastructure built by the homeless for less than a
livable, minimum wage to fully capitalize on the
ability to line their greedy pockets. Proceed to
events like this at your own moral and ethical
peril.

II

Sober, the elevator ride up to the twenty-fourth floor wasn't so bad. With bleary eyes, I had written up my first report and fired it off at my editor like a warning shot across his bow and then ambled out in the clothes I'd slept in. Fortunately, I wasn't trying to make a good impression.

Perhaps the worst thing an editor can do is to send an alcoholic reporter to cover an event completely unsupervised where he'll be able to attend parties. Parties where free alcohol is being handed out to reporters like it was Halloween candy. My press ribbon got me past the bouncer where I was saddled with a gift bag full of crap I didn't need or want with Griffin*Con logos on it. Then I was forced to stand in line for my booze.

"Trick or treat," I said, and was handed a bottle of Corona Extra with a lime. I'm not usually a beer man, but free beer just tastes better. Even swill like Corona.

Bryan Young

I was completely disinterested in the party for anything but free booze, but most press people have the desire to talk to everyone in the room and try to press some type of advantage. With the fact that there was no job security in any newsroom in the country and since freelance was too bloody hard, everyone was on the lookout for a publication that might be their next meal ticket.

The quality of outlets represented in the room was a mixed bag, to say the least. They ranged from local freelancers on assignment with national newspapers and big time bloggers to kids running flyers and websites out of their basements. Though I tried to concentrate on getting drunk, I found it impossible not to stare down at the city below from the floor-to-ceiling window and imagine what it must have been like to be a bird, soaring overhead, watching the city below burn to the ground.

It must have been sad, seeing nowhere to land through the smoke and smolder.

As hard as I tried to keep to my own thoughts, it was impossible. I kept getting dragged out of my head by the pompous voice of an oversized and far too loud black woman being followed around by a pair of high school students with camera equipment. Before I could walk away, she clapped her hand on my back and introduced herself, "I'm Kira Castle, pleased to meet you, sir. I host a little TV show you may have heard of called *Movies With Kira*."

"Never."

"And who are you with, honey bunch?"

"*Titan Online*."

"Oh, dear me, I read that site every day."

38

"I'm sorry. What station did you say your little show was on?"

"Atlanta Public Access. We're just the best little movie show in the South."

"I bet."

"Have you met my husband? Reggie, sweetest, this here is Mister... I don't think I caught your right name."

"My name's Guano."

"This here is my husband, Reggie Castle, Mr. Guano."

She presented to me a completely defeated and grayed old man who seemed on the brink of mental exhaustion. It must have been a chore to keep up with a woman like Kira Castle, even on a slow day.

"Pleased to meet you."

He shook my hand and continued looking distant and uninterested between sighs.

"What are you here covering, Mr. Guano?"

"Oh, this and that."

My ruse to appear boring was working and she was already scanning the room for someone else she should be talking to. When she spotted someone more important to talk to, she handed me her business card that she pulled from the interior of her bra. "Well, it was nice talking to you. If *Titanium* ever needs a movie show, you know right now who to call."

Her cameramen, most likely abducted ninth-graders, followed her about, never once taking their cameras off her. I dropped her card blatantly on the floor and turned back toward the window.

Bryan Young

Five beers and a beautiful sunset later, the party was winding down.

I found myself standing next to a giant swath of Griffin*Con repeater board, but I was too busy drinking and avoiding the grating voice of Kira Castle to notice. My feeling was that it was better to keep my drunken distance than to strangle her.

She was everything wrong with journalism, loud and full of herself; she had no context for anything she talked about and no wherewithal to correct it. She was at best a citizen journalist, a blind person describing a scene out loud to the deaf. The worst part about people like her is the lack of consequences for their actions and the fact that they could blur the line between opinion and fact with all the care of a squatting mule. Sure, maybe she got things right now and again, but if she screwed up so royally at any point she wasn't out anything. There wasn't much of a job at stake and even less self-respect. They could just send falsehood after falsehood out into the ether, ready to be consumed by any old moron who happened by it.

We get something wrong, we catch hell. Some random bitch on public access or some little blog gets something wrong and everyone chalks it up to their status as an amateur. Of course we need to be held by a higher standard, but their access to an audience ready to believe them was enough to make me want to shove my fingers down my throat and vomit all over her.

Sure, I felt like it was ridiculous, but not as ridiculous as the crowd gathering around the girl walking into the party. She was mobbed, for what reason I couldn't guess. She was blonde and plastic, in brand new clothes of a fashion six months out of style. Or six months away from being in style, I couldn't tell which. Either way, it was ugly. From across the room she aroused a feeling of sexual energy in my chest, but as she drew closer, that feeling withered. She glanced at me and doused the fire in my loins as if with a fire extinguisher. Her face bore the marks of beauty in her past, but the outline of her face bore the scars of cosmetic work. The battle plastic surgery had waged had been successful to a point, but you could tell in the long run the battle had become a losing one. I could hear whispers of who she used to be emanating from the crowd. She used to be a star of some TV show or another I'd never seen, played the lead in a movie or two I might have half watched in a drunken stupor.

Feigning a desire to get away from the fawning crowd and flashing cameras, she "escaped" to the repeater board and swatch of red carpet next to me.

The crowd spread out across the border of the carpet beneath her, working hard to make it feel like a standard press event. I didn't care that it was probably imposing on her during a social function, because really, fuck her. I just couldn't stand the idea that out of all of these fucking press vultures, I was the only one who knew how to shut it off for a couple of hours and get a really solid bender going.

Each question they asked her felt like a cheese grater peeling the hair and skin off the back of my neck.

"Since you played the character in the original film but weren't cast in the television show, did that cause any strain on you personally?"

"No, not at all," she paused to pose for a photographer who snapped three quick photos with a flash. I couldn't think of a more vapid question to ask an actress than to ask about a part she didn't get. "I loved what Sarah did with the character, and at that time in my life, I wasn't interested in doing television."

Another photographer stepped in whom she posed for.

Then a phallic microphone was thrust into her face. "Hi, Kirsten? I'm Kira Castle with 'Kira Castle at the Movies,' the biggest little movie show in the South. I'm sure you've heard of us. We were wondering what's next for you?"

Completely oblivious to the function of the microphone, Kira pulled it away from the actress as she answered, "Well, I'm between projects right now, but I'm having a lot of fun on the convention circuit. They like the other stuff I've done, but I was really only on *Star Trek* for two episodes in bit parts, but it's great to see how much the fans still care."

My god.

Taking another slow slip of my drink, I watched morbidly as these two freight trains barreled toward a collision.

"Oh? So you were in the *Star Tracks?*"

In proper form Kira pulled the mic from her before she spoke, "Yes. I played an ensign in two episodes."

"Wonderful. Well, we have our little movie show," she motioned to the pimple-faced teenagers with cameras hovering around her like flies to shit. "And we'd love to have you on and talk to us about the *Star Tracks* and your other shows and what you've got coming up, you can just go ahead and tell us all about it."

Just as she began to answer, there was a rumbling in my stomach. I didn't know if it was her hideous, collagen oozing face or Kira Castle's idiotic line of questioning but I could feel a jet

stream of angry and annoyed liquid rising to the top of my outrage. It wasn't the alcohol in my blood, I've never been affected by
the godly nectar that way. The bilious flow that I choked up and
laid down at the shoes of this "actress" and Kira Castle was a direct
result of their idiocy. I *had* to vomit.

I really didn't have a choice.

It was better than any insulting thing I could have said to
point out their stupidity to the rest of the crowd. It was the most
cathartic vomit I'd ever had.

There was a hand on my back and a voice in my ear, wondering if I was okay. I was better than okay. Watching the two of
them dance in my puke was a glorious site.

"It's glorious!" I told the nagging voice to my side.

Another voice said, "He's had way too much to drink."

Another chimed in, "Is he even supposed to be here? He's
been staring out the window humming 'Flight of the Valkyries' for
the last twenty minutes..."

"That's disconcerting."

Finally, the outrage in my chest ceased heaving and the
stream of stinking vomit stopped growing. The actress and the
alleged movie maven were fleeing the scene in search of somewhere to take off their soiled shoes and pants, shrieking and suppressing vomit of their own.

My boisterous laughter would have been unnerving if everyone hadn't just assumed I was a licentious drunk. A hand
reached down to my back and another under my arm, someone
was helping me get upright. Once back on my feet, I wiped the
excess from my lips with my sleeve and turned to the pair who

helped me up. "Isn't it so much more pleasant in here with those two gone?"

Both were slack-jawed with awe.

"What? Admit it. They were horrible people." It was then that I noticed that the guys who helped me back to my feet were Kira's grade school cameramen. They were too young to contradict me so they just got the fuck out of my way and I left the room. No one wanted to party in a room with a vomit pool in it, so the party was dissipating anyway.

I found a bathroom on the way downstairs and took a long hearty draught of the travel size mouthwash I had in my pocket. Intentional or not, vomit tastes fucking gross.

Hopefully, though, that was the last I'd be seeing of Kira Castle.

The lobby downstairs was filling quickly with convention goers, some in costumes, most with drinks, all looking for a good time and more socializing than I guess they were used to. I suppose everyone deserves to let their hair down occasionally and socialize like proper people. I can't imagine these smelly assholes get many opportunities to wallow in the mire of their own kind and be completely comfortable. Hell, I doubt many of these people were comfortable in their own skins at all.

The first thing I decided to do was to acclimate myself to all the available alcohol in the lobby, which turned out to be quite a bit. Beers and booze could be bought from a refrigerated unit in the gift shop, there were two freestanding, full service bars in the massive open area, and attached to it were two restaurants with bars inside. There was also an additional mezzanine level accessible only by stairs that looked out over the costumed crowd that also served as a bar. I felt like a secret service man checking all of the vantage points and possible points of egress in a building before I got into a situation I couldn't handle.

The plentiful supply of booze made me wonder what sort of event I was in for. Did geeks really need this much to drink? I know I did, but I was a normal person. Were flagons of ale really an integral part of fantasy roleplaying games?

It didn't much matter. My needs would be served easily. In every corner of my hotel lobby I could be served a shot of whatever I wanted and it would see me through this Godforsaken assignment. Maybe not God since I was never one for bearded sky deities. At the very least, it was forsaken by me. Maybe I'm God.

Maybe I have a God complex?

I began my circuit with the mezzanine bar so I could sip some scotch while I got a lay of the land below.

There were easily three or four hundred people in costume alone on the lobby level below me. There were another couple of hundred not in costume, and I'd say about one-third of those below all had cameras and would stop those in the most elaborate costumes to snap pictures. I was additionally surprised by the contingent of women dressed scantily as characters from entertainment franchises I had no recollection of. There were a few I recognized. Princess Leia was one I remembered clearly, and there were at least four women down there dressed in that get up, though maybe only one of them should have been allowed to. The one that should have been allowed to couldn't make it ten feet through the lobby without five people taking her picture, presumably for material to masturbate with. And who could blame them?

I pondered why there was so much traffic in the lobby, wondering where these people could be going, until it hit me: this was the destination. This was the party everyone was going to. I guess it couldn't get any easier than that. Throw your costume on, take the elevator down, and mingle. It wasn't a bad system, I suppose.

I finished off my scotch, ordered another and took my place back at the railing to watch the goings on below. It wasn't a full minute before I noticed a man sidled up to the railing next to me, watching everything with a keen eye and a cocked eyebrow. He was dressed in a red cape with yellow trim and a massive red collar that ended in points above the level of his head. His mustache was black and pencil thin and he wore thick yellow gloves that offset the blue of his tunic. He was at least twenty-five pounds too heavy for the costume, which must have been of a superhero of some sort.

"Who are you supposed to be?"

"Me? I am Dr. Stephen Strange, Sorcerer Supreme, at your service, sir." With a flourish, he produced a business card from thin air. His feat of prestidigitation was impressive, especially considering the thick weight of his gloves. I took the card and he gave me a sign of goat horns with both hands.

"It's a pleasure."

"And what is your name, sir?" He spoke with an arrogant gusto that I couldn't help but like.

"My name's Cobb. I write for *Titan Online*."

"By the hoary hosts of Hoggoth."

"I don't know what that means."

"Don't worry about it. My name's Steve."

"Like the...?"

"Yeah. Total coincidence."

He offered me his gloved hand to shake. "So... Doesn't this thing start tomorrow? Why all the get up now?"

"Why not?"

"That can't be comfortable."

"You know, this is probably the only place outside of Halloween I can wear something this badass and everyone would think it's cool."

"So this is a release for you?"

"I don't know. It's just fun."

"What do you get out of it?"

"Fun."

Maybe it was because I couldn't think of a single thing I did for fun that I tried cutting him down, "You meet women dressed like that?"

"This is my astral projection and has no need for women. My corporeal form at home never dresses like this and has no problems meeting the ladies."

"So, no?"

"No."

"You meet many girls at home?"

"Some. I'm just like anybody else, more shy maybe, but I do okay."

"They run for the hills when they find out you dress as a wizard on the weekends?"

"Dr. Strange isn't a wizard."

"Whatever. She run for the hills?"

"One thought it was pretty weird. A couple got into it."

"Is that so?"

"Well, even if they're not into comic books and sci-fi, every girl likes to play dress up. That's what they all spend so much time doing growing up. What little girl doesn't want to wear all those pretty clothes and costumes and stuff? It's just that some of them outgrow it. And some that don't outgrow it don't like to share it with their men. Others," he waved his hand mystically over the crowd below, "force their men to share it with them. And some of us haven't found anyone to share it with yet."

He sounded like anyone else. Not just a geek. Maybe he was a little bit more like me than I'd care to admit.

He snapped me out of my stupor, "Need another drink?"

"What are you drinking?"

"I've been imbibing of the red wine. Would you like some?"

I didn't want to make eye-contact, but agreed anyway.

With that same flourish, he produced an open bottle of red wine that looked as though it was an antique with no label. He poured me a glass into a plastic cup he'd produced from somewhere and then poured a glass for himself. I was slow to realize that he was pouring his wine into a bejeweled pewter goblet he'd been hiding on his person. Hell, maybe he summoned it forth from another realm. It didn't really matter.

The aged bottle seemed to disappear and I was being handed the cheap cup. He clinked his goblet with mine and drank thirstily. Before imbibing, I sniffed at the beverage and was surprised to find the aromatic hallmarks of a lovely red wine. I'm not an expert in wine and I don't drink much of it, but I knew enough to know this wasn't swill. But was there something up with it? Any man who dresses as a wizard and carries around a prop bottle of wine and his own goblet is not a man to be trifled with. And his work with his hands, manufacturing cards and cups at will, was impressive enough that if he'd slipped something in my drink I'd never know it until it was too late. What if that was the filthy bastard's game? What if this was how he picked up girls, or anything with a hole that could be easily lubricated? Offered them wine, abracadabra, here's a pill, alakazam, I wake up with a mighty sore ass...?

"Everything okay?"

"Just admiring the fragrance."

"Indeed."

With his gaze hot upon me, I figured it didn't matter if he was going to rape me or not. Worst case scenario: I get a nice fat settlement when I sue my employer for sending me into harms way, right? It can work like that. Right?

Bottoms up!

It wasn't bad. A little fruity for my tastes, but it was a pleasant, dry wine.

I never felt intelligent enough to be wine drunk. As I'm sure many of you drunks know, there are different kinds of drunk. Beer drunk is a bit dizzy and a little aggressive. Hard liquor drunk, scotch and whiskey, is hot in your belly and down your throat and gives you just enough of an edge to make you feel like you're Caesar, fallen. Wine drunk is the most intellectual of drunks, and maybe that's why I'm not the biggest wine drinker. I'd read about all the great writers sitting in café's drinking red wine by the barrel and writing masterpieces and maybe I've avoided it because I don't feel worthy. When I sit down to write my novel, then I can afford the intellectual writer's drunk. Until then, it's the fall of Rome for me.

Steve kept filling both our cups, over and over again.

"So this is your first Griffin*Con?"

"It's my first anything con. I'm a political writer. The worthless piece of shit I call an editor sent me out here for his own twisted gratification."

"You said you were from *Titan*, though, right? I thought they cover stuff like this now and again. I remember you guys covered Comic-Con a couple of months ago. There were a couple of articles you guys did about it that I saw."

"Different guy. I'm a hard news man."

"How is this not news? You've got tens of thousands of people in one place, meeting their idols, getting together as fans. There's plenty of celebrities and professionals, lots of interviews and breaking news you could get, I'm sure."

"You really think the entertainment section counts as news?"

"Would people read it if they didn't care at least a little bit?"

Maybe he had a point.

"Besides, you're getting paid for this, aren't you? And I bet they paid for your room. Your press badge was free."

"How much did you pay to be here?"

"Hotels and flights well over a grand. My badge was over a hundred. Plus the grand in spending cash. Shit, man. This is going to cost me two or three thousand, easy. And I'm happy for it. This place is the best."

"We'll see."

"Mark my words. In the end of all things, you'll understand."

He stood, drained the rest of the fluid from his goblet, turned to his ancient bottle and chugged the remnants of that. "I'll see you on the Astral Plane, brother."

With that final, cryptic dispatch, he staggered off, leaving me drunk and confused. I couldn't tell if he disappeared into the crowd or into the Astral Plane.

This whole damn enterprise confounded me and I'd be damned if I didn't get to the bottom of it.

I rose to my feet, hoping my balance wasn't too shot or wobbly for me to make it through this goddamn circus and back to my bed before I collapsed. Perhaps the greater challenge would be making it back to my room without finding myself in a physical altercation. Sure, maybe I was a pacifist, but Jesus Christ some of these costumed bastards looked like they needed to be punched in the face.

By the time I made it down the stairs to the lobby level proper, I realized it had been my intention to do a circuit of all the freestanding bars, and despite the looming threat of alcohol poisoning, I couldn't think of a single compelling reason why I shouldn't carry on. And so I did.

I needed a shot of scotch badly. The crowd was swelled around the bars and I couldn't make heads or tails of where a line started, but that didn't matter since I had no qualms cutting to the front. These people were drinking socially and could wait, but I needed it for my very survival. I was on a desert island looking for my coconut or I'd die of thirst and exposure.

I still had another fifty feet between me and the bar, though, so I got a move on.

"Hey!"

Were they shouting at me? "Who? Me?"

"Yeah. You just walked right through our picture."

I looked around me and noticed the narrow corridor that had opened up and allowed me passage was indeed flanked on one side by a photographer and on the other side by a trio of plastic Stormtroopers and a guy dressed as the shriveled old white guy from *Star Wars*. Waving them off, I kept moving toward my release. I took the advice of one of the guys in fake armour to heart when he said via a loudspeaker in his helmet, "Move along, move along."

"Right-o."

As I took each step closer to the bar, I seemed to get a further and further view of myself from above, as though I could watch all of this happening and I could see the surroundings all around me. Maybe it was the alcohol that disembodied me from the situation, but my gut instinct was telling me that it was just the surreal nature of my surroundings. This couldn't be real life and my mind was illustrating it by giving me an out of body experience. Somehow my brain erased everyone in street clothes from my view and all I could see was the bizarre. To my right there was a masked man in a red and black leotard and ammo bandolier wielding a sword and an orange tipped gun. Behind me was a GI Joe character of some sort. To my left were a group of kids in school uniforms, decked out in gold and red scarves, conducting imaginary orchestras with their magic wands. And in front of me, the last obstacle in the way of my drink, was Abraham Lincoln, replete with goggles, jetpack, and copper, bionic arms.

I tried angling past him, but I couldn't. He stepped in front of me without even having to look.

"Whoa, there, son. There's a line."

"Tell that to John Wilkes Booth."

Lincoln put one bionic hand on his suit jacket collar, as Lincoln would, and the other gently on my shoulder. "There, there, son. Don't be too hasty."

"I just need a drink."

I wanted to avoid eye contact. If he'd survived his assassination and had been rebuilt to last the intervening hundred and fifty years, he could probably kick my ass into oblivion. It probably wouldn't be wise to fuck with old Honest Abe.

"Can I...uh...buy you a drink, Mr. President?"

"No, no," he said in that ridiculously honest voice. "I have my own means, though I do appreciate your offer, kind sir."

Space Lincoln ordered his drink and walked away, giving me a wide berth to order mine. I turned my back and walked a few steps away, terrified he was following me. Who knows what sort of damage those electromechanical arms of his could do to me if he had it in his mind to tear me apart. He beat the shit out of slavery, who the fuck was I?

I turned, spying a peek at Lincoln from the corner of my eye. The crowd around him was rowdy, laughing, and carrying on, but he was still and stoic. Presidential. A photograph trapped in a motion picture. Through those thick black goggles he could have been staring at anything but deep down I knew he was staring at me.

Where were the elevators? Maybe I needed to get out of here.

I was only able to take three steps closer to the elevators before the urge to turn and look once more for my tormentor. It was as before, a photograph in the middle of a moving picture, only he'd moved from the background to the foreground.

"Holy Jesus!"

Guessing that it probably wouldn't help matters, I gulped the rest of my booze, discarded the container on the floor and doubled my pace through the costumed masses. I was moving in slow motion, terrified in a nightmare. Space Lincoln was surely going to kill me for my trespasses and I had to get away.

The button for the elevator blinked on and off every time I pushed it, off and on, on and off. I was frantic.

There was a ding and a door was opening right in front of me. Jumping into the elevator, I sighed deeply. I was safe. I'd been pulled out of harms way. Gazing out the windows, I scanned the lobby floor for any sign of Lincoln. I had the distinct feeling that I was being watched. Slowly, I turned to see that I was alone in the elevator with Space Lincoln.

I pressed my body up against the elevator wall and held my breath, hoping my floor would come up soon.

Confidently, he raised his right hand as if to shake. "You okay, son?"

"Yes," I lied.

I shook his hand, hoping he didn't crush me in his mechanical grip.

"What's your name?" He wasn't letting go.

"My name? Uh... Davis. Yeah. That's it. Jeff. Jeff Davis."

"Pleased to meet you." He shook my entire arm, firmly. It made me wonder if he understood the power inherent in his implants. Surely he must after all this time since his assassination.

The elevator dinged.

"Uh, this is me."

He let go of my hand and took a long, slow draught of his beverage before speaking: "I've got my eye on you, Jeff."

Jesus Christ.

With no grace whatsoever, I turned and fled like a patient in an asylum, straight for my room. I fumbled with the keycard, finally opening the door, and slamming it behind me. The deadbolt system couldn't be engaged fast enough. Would that be enough though? The strength in his one arm could shatter that bolt into splinters. His agents ended the lives of a quarter of a million Confederate soldiers, what the fuck was this deadbolt to him?

I piled the ironing board, my luggage, and the nightstand in front of the door, hoping that might deter him.

And then I collapsed upon the bed...

...blinked...

And it was morning.

Jesus Christ.

Wasn't that the worst kind of sleep? The kind that just disappears in the blink of an eye? The good news was that I had slept off the alcohol in my system and was no longer drunk. On the other hand, the bad news was that I slept off all the alcohol in my system and was no longer drunk.

I checked my watch. 9:00 am. Shit. It was 9:00 am and I was still in Saigon. Every time I think I'm going to wake back up in the jungle out there.

And make no mistake: the lobby out there was a jungle.

Through the door of my room, I could hear the same din of the horde outside as when I came in. The only difference in my room from the night before was the daylight peeking through the curtains. It took me a moment to untangle my luggage from the makeshift barricade I'd erected before my sleepless sleep and I changed my shirt and put on deodorant. At that rate, I figured I'd be cleaner and better kempt than at least ninety percent of the masses outside. Really, who did I need to impress?

Disengaging the dead bolt, I cracked the door open and peeked outside, terrified that I might see Lincoln staring back at me in the hallway. As far as I could tell the coast was clear, so I left my room and headed for the elevators, frequently looking over my shoulder for the ghost of the Great Emancipator.

I squeezed into the packed elevator, a swordfish among sardines, and assumed someone must have hit the right button to get us the lobby by this point. Not that I could reach, or even see, the floor buttons from my position anyway, wedged there between two gargantuan geeks in triple extra large T-shirts and braces. Mentally, I was that swordfish. Physically, I was an algae to their tuna.

From between the stomachs of these geeks, I was birthed into the lobby and staggered as far as I could until I was met with the wall of the crowd. The party had only increased in size since I escaped to my room what felt like only a few moments ago. In this place of surreality, sound sleep would be hard to come by.

Needing something to wake me up and start the process of getting drunk, I began my day seeking out a Bloody Mary. Once I had one, in all of its spicy glory, I left, onward and upward.

I thought it might be best to start my quest for a story on the fringe since I was fresh out of ideas and would have to turn in a story or two by the end of this long, long day. It was then that I noticed the bare, slender legs and well-formed bottoms of two shapely young dames in their early twenties. They were walking against the outer wall, along the edge of the party, heading in a definite direction. They were dressed in short skirts and the garb of sexy, magical school girls, replete with wands and mini-cloaks that came down to their mid-back, drawing all attention to their luscious asses. So what if I was a pervert staring? It was true. Their asses were luscious.

Hell, they'd probably agree with me.

And what better way was there to chase a story than by chasing skirts in the meantime?

Again, I'm a little passive aggressive here. I'll tell myself how mouthwatering these young ladies were, I'd fantasize about all the different ways I'd love to take their costumes off, and I'd play over and over again in my mind what we could do together like some sort of porno film. But would I talk to them? Probably not. If I did, they would probably be the ones asking me a question. Directions most likely. But I could dream, couldn't I? Wasn't that the right and holy prerogative of men? If it wasn't, I'm not sure I'd be able to live in this world, and I'd have to snuff out as many of these bright, twinkling dots of sunshine around me before snuffing out my own.

It wouldn't be pleasant.

Anyway, back to the girls. Their hips swayed and the fabric of their magic costumes could barely contain the sexiness within.

They led me down a path I'd never be able to replicate on my own. Down hallways and corridors, up an escalator, down an escalator, two rights, a few lefts, more rights for good measure. I was beginning to give up on them, assuming they knew as little about their surroundings as I did. But then they committed to a room and entered it. The signage on the front door had four or five panels listed on it at various times. I checked my watch and realized that this was the Harry Potter slashfic panel. Whatever slashfic was, it sounded like a completely made up word, but if those two prime pieces of real estate were interested in it, I'm sure I could find something worth my time. Hell, it might be good for a story.

I opened the door and barged in like a jackass. The door was set at the front of the room by the dais, with hundreds of robed Harry Potter fans staring up at it from the other side. All eyes from the crowd were on me as I walked in, and they followed me as I made my way to the only empty seat in the house. On the front row.

Ignoring them, I settled in and pulled out a notebook, ready to take down everything I'd need to file a story about this slashfic stuff.

There was a moderator who stood at a podium on the dais bearing that silly, self-important Griffin*Con logo. His name was Brayden. The panelists he was moderating sat along a table with small paper placards displaying their names in front of each of them. Their names were not important, but the majority of them were middle-aged women. A couple of them were in costumes of some sort. And there was a young boy there who couldn't be more than eighteen and he was only slightly younger than the moderator.

"Welcome," Brayden began. Apparently the girls and I made it just in time. "This is our third year here at Griffin*Con with the Harry Potter fanfic/slashfic panel and this is my first year moderating, so, uh, please go easy on me."

He flashed a warm smile as the crowd laughed courteously.

"My name is Brayden Jones and I write a pretty popular fanfic you might have heard of, 'The Dramione trilogy'..." The son of a bitch paused for applause and this crowd was stupid enough to give it to him.

"Thank you for that. But today's panel isn't about me. Today's panel is about writing fanfic and slashfic, the legal loopholes you need to jump through to do it, and where to find the inspiration for it. So, without further ado, let me introduce the panel. To my immediate left is Miss Vickie Dean, better known as Silverleaf. She writes Harmony fanfic, including the titillating 'Harmonian Affair.' Then we have Miss Jenny Harwood who writes Puppyshipping Mpreg slash under the nom de plume 'Siriusly.' Next to her is a young man you might recognize from the Youtube sensation *A Very Harry Musical*, James Waits..."

The crowd had offered polite applause for each panelist up to this point, but this James Waits kid got a shrill shriek from every girl in the room, young and old. He may as well have been The King. One bitch even swooned and her friend caught her, I bet. The excitement was leveling off, but he flashed a pop stars smile and the roar of the audience grew deafening.

When Brayden calmed them down, he introduced the last member of the panel: a middle-aged housewife who looked as though at any moment she could die from choking on her own hubris. "And our last panelist is Miss Victoria Jensen. She writes Snarry slash under the name 'HPlovesSS' and is the author of the 'Hogwarts Campout' series."

I thought the reception the kid got was great, but this bitch took the cake. Not as many of the young girls were screaming, but the middle-aged women were going crazy. I'd have to stick around to figure out what the hell all of this was about, but whatever it was, it was catnip to these women. I knew a little about Harry Potter. I mean, who on the planet hasn't heard of it? Wasn't it the single best selling series of books of all time except the Bible? But even a passing familiarity with it couldn't prepare me for all of this mumbo-jumbo.

I was hoping they'd get to the point or I'd have to start asking questions and no one in this room wanted me to start asking questions. Trust me.

"Victoria, let's start with you. When did you first realize you wanted to write slash fiction with Harry Potter and Professor Snape?"

I wrote the term 'slash fiction' down beneath the names of all the panelists, knowing full well I'd probably have to look it all up. My guess? It was Harry Potter slashing up his professor, or the professor getting so pissed off at the little piss-ant that he cuts him up. I could get behind that. Who didn't want that for a release? I must have written a hundred spots of on-the-fly slash fiction of me and my boss.

"Well," she began in a voice dripping in self-importance, "it makes a lot of sense to me. Snape never really got the chance he needed to be with Lily Potter, and she's gone now. And every time he sees Harry he's haunted by this face, I mean, he has her eyes, the facial structure, everything. He's constantly reminded of the love of his life and Harry is this wonderful bright kid. And Snape hasn't really matured since high school and how do you show affection but to torment and tease? It makes so much sense to me."

Did she just say affection?

What the fuck is this?

"And I think with the age that Harry is, and how boyish and effeminate he is, and a man as sexually repressed as Snape, them having a physical relationship is as logical as any other pairing in the slash fiction universe."

"Of all the situations you've written pairing Harry and Snape, what was your favorite?"

"My favorite? I think it might be 'Potions Detention' and it was one where Harry had drawn Snape's fiery ire and was demanded to report to the potions classroom after school and normally there would be at least a few other kids there, but this time it was just Snape and Harry all by their lonesome. And you know that spark when you're alone and there's something you want to say or do that stirs that excitement in you? Well, Snape was full of that. Harry was making a potion, but got it completely wrong and accidentally made a truth potion. Snape tasted it and it hit him. Harry asked him what he was thinking, and Snape was magically obligated to be honest. And it was simple, really. Snape wanted to show Harry what love was and make him cum."

And I thought *I* was a horrible person.

Do you mean to tell me that slash fiction is a term used for writing situations for fictional characters to fuck? That's crazy.

She continued, "I've heard of a few people who have called me out because I've written Harry as someone who is underage in a lot of my stories, though some occur when he's of age, but the simple fact of the matter is that this is fiction. These are fictional characters in a fantasy environment and no children are in danger. Either of reading it, or being preyed upon because of it."

"Horseshit." Apparently, that was me yelling. I hadn't realized that my sense of moral outrage still existed for anything but the downfall of journalism, but here I found it easily boiled over (and largely without my knowledge) in the face of pedophilia.

"Excuse me?" The moderator was incredulous. How dare I just interrupt this panel?

"I said horseshit." I couldn't just keep quiet now. I'd be an even bigger asshole than usual if I didn't stay the course. Say what you will about me, but I'm not a quitter when I mount my high horse. "You're a goddamn pederast, you fucking sow."

"A pederast?" It was Victoria Jensen's turn to be incredulous. "How could I possibly be accused of being a pederast? I've never touched a little boy, nor advocated that anyone should."

"But the thought of that ugly old Professor doing likewise to his student, that little fucking Potter kid, creams your panties like a good old-fashioned rub down and that makes you just as bad as if you were putting your cock in his ass yourself." I was at high volume now. Everyone could hear what I was saying. My guess is that they could all imagine her crusty vagina lubricating itself at the thought of Alan Rickman putting a little boy's cock in his mouth and it made me want to gag.

"I beg your pardon...?" She was clucking now, like a chicken in a hen house, frightened and turning red, puffing her cheeks and flapping her monstrous arms.

"I'm going to expose you, all of you!" I was standing now, in a fury at front of the crowd, motioning to everyone like a mad prophet of doom. "This has got to stop! Who's going to think of the children?"

I've never once thought of the children, but this shit was a bridge too far. This was going to be a good story and people were going to be outraged. I might win a Pulitzer for this. "The world is going to know! They're going to know that Victoria Jensen is a pederast!"

"How dare you? I'm legally protected and it's for entertainment purposes only."

"You're going down, lady. You and all the rest of you perverts."

The moderator came down off the raised platform and led me out of the room with a rough grip on my shoulders. I wanted to leave because this whole enterprise was retarded and disgusting, but I wanted to start a riot. I kept shouting, hoping that someone would carry on for me. To my dismay no one did, though I continued to shout at them, calling them horrible people, and repeatedly invoking the infected, creamy bodily fluids of Victoria Jensen. If I wasn't going to inspire anyone else to act I hope I made at least one of them sick before I was completely escorted from the room.

Once we were out, the moderator, Brayden, cornered me against a pillar. "That was pretty rude, man."

"You're pretty rude."

"Seriously, you totally disrupted our panel."

"Are you saying you want the mouth of a little boy on your cock, too?"

"You need to show a little respect, man. Victoria Jensen is one of the most respected writers of slashfic in the field. I don't have to like her stuff to acknowledge her impact on fan fiction and the slashfic community specifically."

"Do you hear yourself? She writes about a little boy getting fucked by his professor in another author's world. That's not impacting, that's bullshit."

"If you come in there again, I'll have security called."

"Call security. You want to arrest a journalist? History is written by journalists, dickhead. I fucking dare you. I will publicly tear you a new asshole. That's where the power is, not your little fan fiction world. The world will know."

"The world does know. The world likes what we do. You're a crazy person, sir."

Brayden walked back into the room to rejoin the panel, but being the colossal asshole and egotist I am, I had to have the last word. I shouted loud enough that the crowd had to hear me through the door as he passed through it, "You're the crazy one! I'm a sane man in a crazy world!"

But did I believe that?

I had more than enough material to file another story. This would go down in the history books. I'd need to do some research, actually read some of this stuff before I condemn it, but I had more than enough in my notes to burn these little boy fuckers to the ground.

It had happened almost without warning, but I was charged up for the first time. I was enjoying myself. I'd stumbled upon something and it was actually worth reporting. I felt like a new man and I'd blow the lid off all of this bullshit. They would remember me. I was Shiva, created the Destroyer.

There was only one problem: I needed to find my way back to my room so I could write my story and I had no idea where I was. Let's be honest, I was staring at some tail on my way here and wasn't exactly paying attention to the major landmarks.

There were meeting rooms on either side of the hallway I was in and a portal leading to a main arterial walkway in both directions. In short, I was fucked. My destruction of their world would just have to wait until I could find my way back.

I picked a direction and moved, no point in standing still. I was a shark; if I stopped moving, I'd die. Entering the heavy flow of traffic in the hallway, I was surrounded by costumed freaks of all shapes in sizes. A girl dressed as Catwoman distracted my attention. She wore a skintight purple leotard, had a thick mane of black permed hair, and was playing with a bull whip. And was she buxom. My God was she buxom. A comic book with Catwoman in it was the first thing I ever jerked off to, and all of those memories and feelings were rushing back to me, but it all ended when I walked face first into a giant cardboard sword slung over the shoulder of a young female frame.

She could have been cute for all I know, but a massive, oblong, pyramid-shaped helmet obscured her head. Her arms were covered in dried, fake blood and there were splashes of it on her bare torso. I took a moment to consider her torso and wasn't sure what to think. She was slender and soft, but doughy. There was no definition to her stomach. Maybe she was a gamer or something who got no exercise but happened to win the metabolic lottery and was able to stay thin?

When I say her sword was huge, I mean it was massive. It was easily ten feet long and a foot wide. It was made of cardboard, though, so it was easily less than an inch think. Preposterous doesn't even begin to describe it.

She'd realized she'd smacked me in the forehead with her phallic weapon and seemed to be trying to apologize to me, but I couldn't make out the words she was saying beneath her mask.

"Hey, you know which way to the Marriott lobby?"

She mumbled something else.

"Marriott. Lobby. Do you know where it is?"

The triangular construct bobbed up and down as though she was trying to nod her head affirmatively.

"The Marriott Lobby. How do I get there?"

She said something else, but I couldn't make it out.

"Just fucking point in the direction of the Marriott Lobby, please."

Raising her arm, slowly for dramatic effect, she pointed with a bloodied finger back behind her, in the direction I was heading. If her word was to be believed, she was setting me on the right track. Who knew if these damn kids were ever telling the truth? If they were at a Con like this they were obviously content to lie to themselves about a lot of things, why not keep up the tradition with a poor and helpless stranger?

Bastards.

Herded by the masses, I found myself unable to break direction from them. Various cordons kept us all moving in the same direction without deviation, almost as though we were in a queue at a bloody amusement park. My guess was that the escalator coming up quickly was heading in the wrong direction, but I was pressed up against a wall and didn't seem to have much choice, so I ascended it.

The escalator brought me up to the lobby of a hotel I'm reasonably sure I'd never been to. It was disconcerting since I was positive I'd never left my hotel.

This lobby was tiled everywhere in a cheap ceramic imitation of Italian marble. People were loitering everywhere. It was exactly the same scene, filled with the same people, as the view from my hotel room, only smaller. Off to my left was a bar, open and ready for my business. Surely the bartender could offer me directions and a shot of a stinging, delicious brown liquid.

Unlike before, there was no line for alcohol and there were empty stools at the bar. I sat down next to a trio of Stormtroopers taking a rest with their helmets off, imbibing mimosas. Maybe it was just orange juice, but if it were me running around in a black leotard and thirty pounds of white plastic armour, I'd need to be drinking constantly.

They couldn't quite sit on the stools. They all sort of leaned on them. Their full, considerable weight on the hard stools would almost surely crack their ass armour, and they couldn't have that happening now, could they?

I flagged the bartender. "Whiskey."

A voice from the chair to my other side said, "That's my line."

"Huh?" I turned to see that I was sitting next to Indiana Jones.

"Whiskey. It was a joke. That's what Indy asks Marion for in the bar in Nepal. Then he cracks that guy's head open with the bottle."

"Ummm."

"It's such a great movie."

"Uh-huh."

I sipped at my drink, trying to ignore this guy, but it wasn't possible. He was simply too enthusiastic about his costume.

"Can you guess which Indiana Jones I am?"

"The Harrison Ford one?"

"Ha. No, from which movie?"

"No idea."

"I'm from The *Temple of Doom*. See? I've got the long sleeve shirt with the rips in it. I spent so much time looking for one, but I could never find the right one, so I made it myself."

"I bet." I took another sip of my whiskey and turned to the guys in the armour, hoping they'd do a better job ignoring me.

They were deep in their own conversation and no matter how inane it might be, it couldn't be worse than the professor here talking to me.

"I'm telling you, Jerjerrod was a rebel spy."

"How could he be? It doesn't make any sense."

"It makes perfect sense. Think about it, who is the only person Vader told that the Emperor was going to be on the Second Death Star?"

"Jerjerrod."

"And what's the vital piece of information Mon Mothma drops in the briefing to the rebels?"

"That they'd discovered that Palpatine was going to be on the Death Star during their assault."

"Think about this, okay, why would they show us Vader telling Jerjerodd about that when we were going to see Palpatine arriving anyway, if we aren't meant to assume he was the leak of the information?"

"But if Jerjerrod was a rebel spy, why would Palpatine put him in charge of the Death Star?"

"Don't you see? This is the beauty of the plan. What is Palpatine known most for?"

"Force lightning?"

"No. For meticulous plotting of plans that are forty steps removed from his goal. That's why they called him 'The Phantom Menace.' He wanted the rebels to know he'd be there and putting Jerjerrod in charge was his insurance policy that they'd know it. If they knew Palpatine was there, they'd be sure to throw everything they had to offer at him so he could smash it in his trap."

Over my shoulder, Indiana Jones shouted, "It's a trap!" for some reason.

"I guess that makes sense."

"Of course it makes sense. Palpatine was fucking brilliant. It's not because of his plan that we lost. It's because Vader was a goddamned traitor."

Jesus Christ.

I wonder what these guys could accomplish if they applied their analytical thinking to real world problems. I couldn't abide my silence any longer, "Was it your mother's meticulous plan to prevent you from getting laid by forcing you to watch these movies over and over again as a child?"

All three of them turned to consider me blankly. One even blinked with the slow comprehension of a moron.

Finally, the one who spent his time theorizing about rebel spies in his midst fired back, "Hey, go fuck yourself, pal."

Without breaking eye contact with him, I blasted the rest of my whiskey down my throat, slammed the glass down on the bar and threw a wad of bills on the counter.

"You're still not going to get laid dressed like that. Jackass."

I walked away.

Sure they were laughing at me, but I was still right and they were still jackasses.

Their snickering is what made it twice as embarrassing when I came back to ask the bartender for directions back to the lobby of the Marriott.

They laughed even more and I wondered if I had enough violence in me to cause them some sort of hurt if they tried anything. It didn't take long for me to run enough scenarios in my head to realize that I'd need a spear or a gun to cause them any discomfort in that armour. Maybe a spear gun, even. I imagined myself dressed as one of those little teddy bears that routed them in that battle they were talking about, throwing rocks at one, hurling a blunt club at another and stabbing the other with a spear in that black space between his chest plate and his helmet.

Assholes.

I passed through the archway the bartender pointed me toward to find myself passing a bank of elevators, down a minor set of stairs, and into a mall food court.

What the fuck?

I was never going to be able to file this damn story.

This food court looked different from all of the other parts of the convention in only that everyone was seated. The heaping portions of greasy food, set out in front of the geeks who'd decided this was the time and place to fill their gullet, consumed just about every available piece of table space in the dining area. Half of the geeks were in costumes, at least. A *Star Trek* guy here, a tattooed something or other there, a girl in an ornate dress in that direction, a Princess in a metal bikini over in this direction.

There was no shortage of creativity in this place. I had to give them that.

It was another hour and a half before I finally found my way to the lobby of my hotel and its familiar red and beige pallor. I had expected the crowd to wane with the passing of midday. There were panels and presentations and exhibit halls and speeches they should have all been attending, but there was no break to the crowd. The lobby was still filled with costumed savages to the point where just looking at it gave me a sensation of vertigo. I was in the middle of a wild animal park. I was a sandaled Roman stepping carefully through a den of sleeping lions toward the elevator. Dizzied, I could trace the sinking feeling in my stomach floating up to my chest, making me wonder if I'd make it through all of this with my life intact. If any of these goddamn animals woke up, aware of my presence, my heart might explode from fright.

My blood pressure skyrocketed as I made it to the bank of elevators and all I could think of was that I wanted to talk to Laurie one more time and tell her I loved her before these man-eating swine ate me alive.

Ding! The elevator doors opened and he was there, standing in the lobby just on the other side of the glass of the elevator.

Space Lincoln.

Last night was not a dream. Through his menacing black goggles I could tell that he was looking directly at me. A fiendish smile crept across his lips when he realized who was standing there in the elevator, frantically pushing the button for the ninth floor. He must have been imagining what horrible things he would do to me when his lips parted, baring his sharp, yellowed teeth.

The speed of my heart outpaced a racehorse when I noticed that in Lincoln's hands he held the most fanciful, steam powered firearm I had ever seen. Tubes and hoses ran from his jet pack and directly into the side of the gun.

He could vaporize me without a second's hesitation and I would be obliterated into bits of matter, never to be seen or heard from again.

I held my breath, waiting for him to end it all until the elevator door whooshed shut. As I rose in the elevator, he never broke eye contact with me until he disappeared below and could no longer see me.

That was too close for comfort.

He must have taken me seriously when I told him I was Jefferson Davis and now he was out to get me. With a vengeance.

Back in the safety of my room, I doubled the strength of my barricade and dialed Laurie on the phone. I knew full well it would cost me a fortune, but hearing her voice would be worth it.

"Laurie?"

"Yeah."

"How's things?"

"Fine. Why? What's wrong?"

"Nothing's wrong. Why would something be wrong? I just wanted to call and say hi."

"You never call. Not unless something's wrong. What did you fuck up this time?"

"I didn't do anything. I just needed to talk to you."

I could hear a man's voice in the background asking who it was, and I could hear Laurie telling him to shut his mouth. "Why?"

"Why what?"

"Why do you need to talk to me? I'm a little busy at the moment. Can it wait till later?"

"Well, I just... I was thinking about starting to work on my novel again..." Why was I so helpless and searching for words? What was wrong with me? I was never without something to say.

I could hear the vague echo of a sucking sound in the background. My blood boiled, but I tried to keep my cool.

"I just... I really just needed to hear your voice. This assignment is killing me. In every way it's killing me. This place is crazy."

"Crazy?"

Bryan Young

"A bionic Abraham Lincoln is trying to kill me."

"Listen, Cobb, I don't have time for your delusions right now. I'm busy right now. Can I call you back later? I promise I will."

"Laurie..."

She hung up.

"...I love you."

I placed the receiver gently back into its cradle. She wasn't going to call back. She was probably sucking some other guy off. Maybe a host of guys.

Restraining my jealousy, I reminded myself that it was probably my fault. It was me that pushed her away somehow. And this job was killing me. Not just the part of it here that I was dealing with in Atlanta, the whole thing.

Curling up in the fetal position on the bed, I can assure you that I did *not* sob like a little baby.

PEDOPHILES AMONG THE GEEKS!
By M. Cobb

ATLANTA, GA -- "Snarry" is not a term that most
people know. For some in the Griffin*Con-going
crowd, it is a secret, sexy, and disgusting code
word for their vile pedophilic fantasies. A
combination of names taken from the Harry Potter
series by British novelist J.K. Rowling,
"Snarry" is short hand for fan written fiction
stories that see Professor Snape (played in the
films by Alan Rickman) and Harry Potter (Daniel
Radcliffe) congressing each other sexually in
tawdry and contrived situations.

The world's premiere "author" of these torrid
fictions is one Victoria Jensen, who writes on
the Internet pseudonymously as "HPlovesSS." She
appeared on a panel at Griffin*Con to explain
her sick obsession, "As a somewhat lonely,
middle-aged woman, I find that writing about the
sexual exploits of Professor Snape and Harry
Potter together is an incredibly liberating en-
deavor, sexually speaking, of course."

One story by Jensen involves the sodomy of the
minor child by his Hogwarts Professor using
cooking oil as lubricant. Another involves the
older man orally stimulating the young boy's
genitals while masturbating.

Though the author claims a first amendment right
for the stories and insists that although the
sexual acts depicted in the stories are indeed

pedophilia, they do not violate child pornography laws. *Titan* will be leading a full investigation of the legality of this issue.

Though Bloomsbury Press, the original publisher of the Harry Potter series, could not be reached for comment, it must be assumed that they are already seeking legal remedies against the diseased mind of Victoria Jensen and those like her.

An official Griffin*Con spokesperson was also unavailable for comment for the purposes of this story. It is unclear why they would offer such a platform for the spread of such real and quantifiably horrible child pornography.

III

I wasn't sure if I could face going out there again. Nothing outside that door was easily understood. Pedophiles roamed free alongside bionic ex-Presidents. Nothing made sense. Up was down, left was right, water was wine, scotch was whiskey.

It was all so damned topsy-turvy.

Staying locked up in my room and going on one of my legendary benders seemed like a wonderful idea. At least it would be comfortable. But I couldn't afford my usual agoraphobic behavior and go on an alcohol binge. Sure, I'd be going on an alcohol binge anyway, but I needed to be out there collecting stories. As shitty as this job was, it was still a job. Uncovering that kiddy porn ring had given me a jolt of satisfaction so maybe there were some other travesties lurking about that I could expose the cleansing light of journalism to.

Bryan Young

The map in the events guide listed three different exhibition halls. I couldn't even fathom what sort of sci-fi themed auto-erotica might be on display for the perverted and sexually repressed masses that this sort of event obviously attracts. But I'm a reporter. Finding out about things I couldn't even begin to comprehend is my fucking job.

Sure, I wanted to leave neither the comfort of my room nor the bottle of Bushmill's under my pillow, but there was territory to chart and gold to plunder. If I could muster the courage I could be Columbus, discovering the new world. Of course there are people here that know all of what there is to know about this savage land, but I'm discovering it for the part of the world that matters.

I'd navigate my way to one of the exhibition halls, which seemed like as good a place as any to find a story. Maybe I'd find a people to enslave to search for gold and virgins on my behalf like Columbus did. At this rate, though, I'd never find it. For his incompetence, the convention's cartographer deserved to be dragged into the middle of the street and have his hands cut off like an Iranian thief. The map looked the same from every angle and the newsprint smudged easily, collapsing the lines in on each other until it was nearly incomprehensible.

It looked more like a scorched circuit board than a map.
Fuck.

I was tempted to light the damn thing on fire but opted against it. Normally, I wouldn't care about burning the building down, but I had no idea where the stairwells were. Rule number one for horrible behavior is to know where the exits are.

Unbelievably, the size of the crowd in the lobby had swelled. Would it ever reach a point of critical mass? It was astounding to me that a fire marshal hadn't arrived to just send everyone back to their parents' basements. Then again, if I were a fire marshal, I wouldn't mind if most of these people were being roasted alive in the event of a fire either.

I stopped a guy walking past me, he was dressed in red sweatpants and a matching red beanie. He wasn't wearing a shirt and all of his exposed skin was painted sky blue. His beard appeared to be spray painted white. He smelled like body odor, chemicals, and bad decisions.

Maybe he was a Martian or something, I didn't ask. I didn't know and I really didn't care. All I needed was a nudge in the right direction to find the ever-elusive exhibit hall.

"Well, which one are you looking for?"

"The exhibit hall."

"I know. Which one?"

"The one with things on display and geeks slobbering all over all of it."

"There's like three of them in the building."

"It's in the building we're standing in?"

"Yeah."

"Where?"

"There's two one floor down, and I think there's another one on the floor below that. I'm not totally sure."

"This your first rodeo?"

"No. This is my third con."

"After three cons, you can't tell me where the exhibit hall is?"

"It's not really my bag."

"But you're sure that if I head downstairs, I'll find the exhibit hall?"

"One of them, yeah."

Involuntarily, I made a noise that was somewhere between a sigh and a disgusted moan.

"You're welcome?"

I let him go on his merry blue way without acknowledging him again. I still wasn't sure if he'd actually helped me or not, especially given the fact that the down escalator he'd pointed me toward had a considerable line.

Jesus. Even the escalators in this place had a fucking line. Didn't anyone believe in the free flow of people?

Apparently not.

Ten minutes later I finally found myself on the right floor and sure enough there were lines to get into the rooms. There was a line to peruse a wall of poorly executed art along the back. Beside that, there was a line for an ATM machine. There was even a line to get into the can. The lines for the exhibition hall were both about the same length, so I picked the one closest to me and dove in.

For once, I was wedged between two people in plain clothes and backpacks. They seemed like completely reasonable people, not at all what I was used to. We all inched closer and closer to the door but neither of these guys possessed the skills needed to strike up a conversation. So I did it for them. I chose the one behind me to start with. He was wearing a billowing pair of khaki cargo shorts and a large T-shirt that said, "It's not going to lick itself." His hands remained locked on the straps of his backpack.

"So, why are you here?"

He pretended not to hear me. I glanced casually to make sure he wasn't wearing headphones and tried again.

"Is this your first convention?"

Again, nothing.

This time, I waited to speak until he locked eyes with me.

"Why aren't you listening to me?"

"Huh, what?"

"I was asking if this was your first convention."

"Oh. No. I've been to tons of conventions. Not Griffin*Con, though. This is my first one."

"Why did you come this year?"

"I don't know. I like cons."

"Obviously. But why do you like them?"

"They're awesome. I get to hang out with people who get me. Meet cool people, that kind of stuff. I met Alex DeLarge earlier. That was awesome."

The line was nearing the door and I was only going to get one more question out of this guy, so I had to make it count.

"You ever get laid coming to one of these?"

We were through the doors and I was convinced that he was going to answer my question, but his eyes widened and he just walked away.

Left alone to resume my mission, I took in my surroundings. The exhibit hall was much smaller than I would have guessed for an event this size. The room was filled with aisle after aisle of black-draped tables with merchandise on them. For the most part, the vendors were selling collectibles, games, toys, posters, and things of that nature. There were a few major corporate brands presenting their wares no one cared about. Well, plenty of people cared about them, but I just walked right by them, raising my nose in the air.

This sort of event must keep the blacksmiths of the world in business. It wouldn't surprise me to find out that conventions were one of their few viable markets. One blacksmith there seemed to be running an entire armory. There were a hundred swords on various racks, all made of thick steel and other alloys, and in various makes and models. Some of the swords seemed to be from actual franchises and had licensing built into them.

"What's the story with this sword?"

"That's the Master Sword."

"A master sword?"

"No. It's the Master Sword. You know? From *Zelda*."

"I was not aware."

A guy dressed in a black and red leotard from head to toe with a machine gun strapped to his back and a pistol strapped to his side was trying out different katanas at the booth. Each time he drew a sword, practicing, he'd let out an ugly sound.

Apparently, he needed just the right one.

His mask obscured every detail of his face. It made me wonder about the safety of this place. I'd seen at least three other guys dressed identically to this clown. There were probably a dozen guys of varying shapes and sizes roaming the convention center in the exact same costume and it made me wonder about my safety.

Say this guy does buy one of these swords. He's got it all day. He's in a mask. For arguments sake, what happens if he wants to commit something like a murder? He's in a costume, there are a dozen other people in the same costume. The mask and gloves obscure all of their distinguishing characteristics. What if they decide to run a bitch through?

What would a witness tell the police? "It was a masked man with a sword."

The cop would just turn around, look and see that everyone in this nuthouse was wearing a mask and wielding a sword. How do they even begin to start an investigation for that sort of crime? Do they perform thousands of interviews and end up just chalking the death up to the nature of the con? It seems like that's all they could do.

The prospect of such an easy to get away with murder sounded incredibly attractive. I could feel my sword hacking into the meat and bone of an anonymous neck seam. It worried me because it felt good.

Soon, blood was everywhere and I was eating the raw flesh like hamburger. It was bizarre and disgusting.

Snapping myself out of it, I moved on from my morbid fantasies and went looking at other booths on the exhibition hall floor.

There was one that got my attention, not for the merchandise it was selling, but for the utter beauty of the girl working the table. She was blonde, freckled, and slight of frame. Her face was plain, but cute, and she wore a tight black corset that created a mesmerizing effect with her breasts. I couldn't take my eyes off of them. Her. I couldn't take my eyes off of her.

Bryan Young

I found myself standing a row of people back and watching this intricate dance go on, as if I were watching a scripted drama. They made this very room a theatre with such expert play-acting.

The two guys in front of me seemed normal enough. Both had conservatively short hair. One wore blue jeans, the other gray slacks and a backpack.

They were trying to buy something or another, it looked like a snow globe with Darth Vader in it, and they were talking to the corseted young minx about their transactions.

"I want to get that globe."

"And I'd like to get this." The other fellow lifted up a T-shirt from the table.

When she spoke, it was with a ridiculous, fake British accent. It was something I would have expected to hear at a Renaissance faire. "All right, let me find out how much with tax."

I was beginning to think things were reasonably straight-forward in this corner of the convention until the pretty young lady was interrupted by a low voice that squeaked with a flux of hormones. "Uh, hi..."

"Hold on one-second, please?" She dealt with her customers, giving them their change, and then she turned her attention to the boy. Calling him a boy was probably too generous. He was easily in his mid-twenties. With my vast powers of stereotyping, I guessed that he was unemployed and living in a basement, his only pleasure in life was the video games he played and magazines he jerked off to. Do kids jerk off to magazines anymore? I guess in this day and age they do it all on their computer.

Fucking kids these days.

Lost at the Con

I was fascinated by the possibilities of what this train
wreck of a boy held. The rising bulge in his sweatpants told me
that he was smitten with this girl and his eyes couldn't decide if
she was a face or a disembodied pair of breasts.

I grinned. A front row seat for an encounter of this mag-
nitude was a blessing.

"Okay, what did you need, sir?"

"Yes, I would like to know how much that Musha Cloth
Heavy Weapons Gundam behind you is." His voice could only be
described as nerdy: nasally and unsure despite the matter-of-fact
tone. He pointed at a massive gray and red box behind her that
looked like it could fit four or five board games inside of it.

"That one's two hundred and thirty. Would you like to
see it?"

"No. I have a friend who has one. He already built it, I
know what it's like."

"Uh-huh."

"I think I might get it. My parents owe me the money."

It seemed painfully obvious he wanted to impress her
with his story, but where could this possibly be leading?

"Oh." She smiled at me, hoping I'd save her.

Not a chance.

"You see, I need to babysit my grandfather this weekend
and they owe me money for that."

She asked me if I needed anything, but he didn't hear her
so he didn't stop.

"He's 94."

87

This was getting really good. But could he possibly make things worse? This girl was clearly not interested in him, but he was working his hardest to woo her.

"He's incontinent and doesn't like to wear adult diapers."

Holy shit.

The cashier blushed, making eye contact with me, not the boy and his shit-filled story. Fortunately for her, he couldn't possibly get any worse. Just as I was about to ask her whether or not she was worried about potential rapists, he injected once more, "Somebody has to clean up that mess. And they pay me to do it. I make a lot of good money doing it."

Completely disarmed, her hands dropped to her side, unable to concentrate on me or anything else.

"Yeah. I've already spent like four hundred bucks at this con. Two-thirty for that thing is nothing. I think I'll get that Gundam. I just need to ask my parents. Maybe I'll be back."

"Oh. Okay." Sheepishly, she watched the kid walk away without any reasonable segue or goodbye. Social skills were not a thing he learned in his years of cleaning up geriatric shit.

I actually felt bad for the girl. Her face was flushed and red, her eyes were darting about, not sure of herself. She laughed nervously, trying to let some of the emotion escape.

"Does that happen to you often?"

"Not really?"

"You're not hit on a lot at a place like this? I imagine it's crawling with sexual repression."

"Oh, I get hit on a lot, but I don't think anybody's ever tried hitting on me by talking about how good they are at cleaning up poop."

"It's not normal."

"Did you want to look at anything?"

"No. I just had a few questions for you. Press."

She noticed my badge but didn't care. "I don't think I'd have much to say."

"Well, you could tell me how you get treated. Pretty young girl like you at a place with all of these completely clueless jag offs, must not be easy."

"It's fine, though. That was just one weird guy."

"How many of those do you get in a day, though?"

"I don't know. One or two perhaps?"

"And what's with the accent?"

"My accent?"

"What is it? It screams like faux-Renaissance fair or something."

"My dad is British, my mom is from the South. I'm somewhere in between."

"So that's not fake?"

"No."

"Oh."

She turned to the person next to me and helped him in to an overpriced toy he could take home and jerk off on.

I left the exhibition hall feeling more and more confident I'd get one of those full body costumes and a sword before the end of this convention. Well, I got in line to leave the exhibition hall at least. It was another ten minutes before I was finally able to make my escape. You had to give it to these geeks. They really did know how to leave a room single-file and in an orderly fashion.

Bryan Young

Conveyed upwards on the escalator, I was left to consider myself in a world I didn't understand. I looked down at my appearance, realizing I truly didn't fit in here. I was slim in a sea of mostly fat people (though there were plenty of exceptions). I wore khakis and loafers in a sea of stretch pants, spandex, and jeans. I wore a shirt that buttoned at the front over a plain white undershirt in a sea of comic book character logos, *Star Wars* characters, and costume shirts. I carried a bag slung over my shoulder full of notebooks, pens, and information, where everyone else was carrying fake weapons and escapism.

What would ever make me feel like I could fit into a place like this? Sure, I liked stuff like this when I was a kid, but I left all that behind me.

Now, I was alone wherever I went. Solitude was the default setting in my life. I worked alone at my cubicle, talking as little as possible to anyone else, cutting myself off from everyone. At home, Laurie treated me as an absent roommate, even when I was home. At the bar no one spoke to me about anything other than what I was drinking. Among my peers I had no one I commiserated with. My misery was a singularity to my life and work.

And so I continued, on and up the escalator, surrounded by people, but absolutely and utterly alone.

The scene in the lobby at the Marriott had not changed since my sojourn into the bowels of the convention hotel. The only major difference was a gaggle of massive, brightly colored costumes, constructed of god knows what, sprouting up over the heads of the regular sized crowd.

A hand on my shoulder aroused me from my stupor of self-loathing.

"Hey, you're the guy who tore Victoria Jensen a new asshole this morning."

"What?"

The pair of young girls I'd so lecherously followed to my Harry Potter story stood before me, shaking me back into consciousness.

"You really going to write that article?"

"Huh? Oh. Yeah. I tapped it out and sent it in to my editor already."

The girls giggled. From the front they weren't that bad looking. They were shaped better than anything else. They were in their early twenties, it seemed, but both obviously had a penchant for young adult fiction. They were still dressed in their schoolgirl costumes and I spent my time biting my lower lip to prevent an erection.

The blonde introduced herself first. "I'm Jessica, what's your name?"

She passed her wand off to her left hand and offered to shake my hand with her right. She looked very much like a Jessica: not ugly but not incredibly attractive either. Another few points of alcohol in my blood and she could pass for Grace Kelly.

I shook her hand, wishing for a drink.

"Cobb."

Her dark haired friend smiled at me and offered her hand, too. "I'm Katie."

Katie looked like a movie star without the plastic surgery. She was the girl next door. Freckles were splashed across her face as though they were flicked from the end of a horsehair brush, no two alike in size or opacity. She was captivating.

Since they were both reasonably attractive, I had to assume they were underage and this was some sort of sting operation. With caution is how I would proceed.

"What can I do for you?"

"We just wanted to say thanks for standing up to that bitch." I'd forgotten their names already and couldn't tell you which one said that. I guess it was probably Katie, she was the last one to shake my hand, right?

"If everybody hates her so much, why is she on a panel?"

"She's well respected and her stuff really isn't that bad. We just can't stand her personally."

"Then why did you go to her panel?"

"Well, we go to all the Harry Potter panels."

"Even though you knew this one was about pedophilia?"

"It wasn't all about that, most of the stories happen after Harry's eighteen. And you left before they started talking about the Draco-Hermione 'shipping."

"I don't know what that means."

They both giggled.

"You really are new around here, aren't you?"

"This has been the single most bizarre experience of my life."

They giggled again.

Apparently they thought I was hysterical and cute in a helpless sort of way.

"You're a reporter though. Don't you do stuff like this all the time?" It was the blonde one talking now.

They were so full of sugar and lollipops that any extended exposure was sure to give me cavities. "I had no idea anything like this even existed. Quite frankly, it seems bottom of the barrel."

"Why is that?"

"I've seen things."

They both said, "Like what?" at exactly the same time. I expected them to both bob up like cheerleaders, giving their breasts enough lift to make me salivate.

"I've seen the depths of depravity in the human character. Not just the pedophilia incident, but the worst kind of mouth-breathing geeks and basement dwelling role-players. This is a cesspit of stereotype. And that's not even mentioning the fact that I think an ex-President is here and trying to kill me."

"What?"

"Nothing. Never mind. Suffice to say it's been a bad experience."

"Sounds like you've only run across the nerds and the weirdos."

"There's another kind?"

"Well, we don't seem like weirdos or nerds, do we?"

"You're both dressed up as Harry Potters."

"You think we should put on more clothes?" That was the dark haired one. Katie? She did a twirl in her too-short skirt.

"On the contrary..."

They laughed again. With me. Not at me.

I couldn't understand the genuine warmth these girls were exuding toward me. It wasn't something I was accustomed to.

I don't know if you can tell, but I'm not exactly a likeable character.

This was something I could get used to.

They asked me a dozen more questions about the sort of things and people I had encountered since I'd been there and they did something that truly surprised me. They offered to show me the nightlife of Griffin*Con. Convinced that I'd only seen the worst parts with the most stereotypical denizens of Griffin*Con, they wanted me to see it as the real people, the normal people, the genuine people saw it.

How would this end?

"How do you know I'm not some kind of rapist or serial killer? I could be anybody. Look at me."

It was getting a little disgusting that every damn thing I said was met with a fucking giggle.

"I'm sure we'll be okay." The blonde one. Jessica? She flicked her wand at me.

"I'm going to require plenty of liquid courage before I go anywhere with you two. And I'll give a fair warning: as coarse as I am now, with enough liquor in me fucking forget about it."

Fucking giggles.

You'd think they were attracted to antisocial, sociopathic behaviour.

"We've got beer and tequila in the room." Jessica, the blonde one, made a motion with her hands that simulated the pouring of this libation down her gorgeous throat.

"You two have gone fucking sideways."

I bet you could guess what their reaction to that was. My ears must have been deceiving me because I could have sworn these two impressionable young ladies just invited me up to their room.

There was a nagging sensation in my chest that weighed down all the way into my gut and added pressure onto my loins and bladder. It was a feeling that told me this adventure probably wasn't going to end any better than anything else I could do this trip. At least there would be pretty faces to look at, I suppose.

"What exactly are we doing?"

Once more in unison: "Room party."

This must truly be the Mardis Gras of geekdom... Nerdis Gras? This was getting ridiculous. What would they want to bother with me for? It didn't make sense. But could I argue? Isn't this what the American Dream had become? We all wanted to be invited up to a room for drinks and who knows what by a pair of lovely coeds. Working damned hard for that picket-fenced two-story in suburbia wasn't enough of a dream anymore. We wanted debauchery. All of us. At the end of the day, debauchery had installed itself as the new American Dream.

It happened while none of us were looking.

My guess is Paris Hilton put it there sometime in 2004.

It'll be hell getting that stain off of Uncle Sam's pinstripe suit.

Fuck it. If this was the dream, I'd live it. And the best part was that I was getting paid to live it. I'd tear myself a new asshole of debauchery. I'd be leaving fecal traces of my sins smeared all over this godforsaken town and it would feel good.

My only reservation about this dream, as great as it was, was that it wasn't *my* dream.

But it didn't matter. So I told them to lead the way to the party.

And they did.

For just a moment, as I watched them swagger in front of me, I forgot entirely about Laurie.

I'd have time to deal with that ulcer-waiting-to-happen later.

The room they led me to was on a floor of the Marriottt somewhere in the teens. Their room wasn't a suite, but it had two beds and was much wider than my room. Unlike mine, which was somewhere below us (I think), this room was home to at least twenty people. How they fit inside comfortably was completely beyond me, but somehow they managed.

Before we walked beyond the threshold of the door, I stopped the girls, hoping to get information of any sort before I would probably lose them for good in the chaos of the room party.

"Is this your room?"

"No." Katie turned to talk to me. Jessica hadn't noticed or cared that I had a question and carried on into the room.

"Whose room is this, then?" I didn't care to know for my sake, per se, but in case I got a story out of this, it would be good background.

"I dunno."

"How'd you find out about this thing?"

"Text from a friend." Katie smiled coyly at me and raised up her cell phone, as if I wasn't familiar with a device of that nature. The real question was where she'd been keeping it in that outfit. My guess was that she had a secret, extra pocket in her vagina or something.

Gross, sure, but also somehow arousing.

There wasn't much more information I could glean from these two, and they seemed more interested in getting us all in to the party than talking with me about shit that didn't matter. Who could blame them?

I wouldn't want to talk to me if I didn't have to either, especially with booze and depravity so close on the horizon. So, in we went.

The party was standing room only.

Both beds were full of lounging, drinking, merrymakers. I made eye contact with a girl with green eyes. Her face was framed beautifully by her hair that was long, straight, and forest green. She was taking a long, slow drag from a hookah that she held in hands draped in white, arm-length gloves. The sinewy cord connected to her pipe ran down the front of her over her green trimmed sailor costume and beyond her green miniskirt and through her perfect legs. Tantalizingly, the cord came out behind her and up to the giant hookah that stood like the Washington Monument in between the two queen beds. The smoky tower cast a faint crimson glow the color of its glass across her backside, giving her a line of red light that made me wonder what it would be like to actually see this girl in a red light district.

Snapping out of it, I maneuvered as fast as I could through the crowd. I managed to make my way to the windows at the back of the room. There was some cheap paperback I read one time where the bad-ass protagonist would enter a room and always head for the back, facing the crowd. He was an assassin or covert operator or something, the details were lost on me, I must have read the book as a kid, but he talked about how naked he felt with his back exposed to strangers and in a room like this, he'd always get his back to a wall or a corner so he could keep an eye on everyone. In his case, it had a lot to do with the fear of being killed, a knife plunged into his back at only a moments notice. In my case, it probably had a lot to do with a subconscious desire not to be hurt or abandoned.

Secretly, I've always been terrified that I'd have my back turned, enjoying my drink and singular existence, only to turn around and find that I was all by myself. I was so disposable in the grandest of schemes that no one would have even bothered to let me know that the party had moved elsewhere.

Maybe I needed to work on my confidence.

Fuck me.

So there I was, pressed with my back against the red curtains and the window, casting my eyes across the room wondering where I could get my first and most gorgeous hit of alcohol at this room party.

Apparently, I had already solved this problem: I looked down to see a bottle of beer and a wax cup full of Jager in my hands.

I really needed to work on my short-term memory for stuff like that. Can you blame me? That girl on the bed was fucking mesmerizing.

The girls I'd arrived with were deep in conversations on either side of me and I was starting to get uncomfortable. My social anxiety was returning. It started like a painful warmth in my solar plexus and felt like it was going to come up as indigestion.

Time for the Jager.

Down the hatch!

That helped calm the feeling a little. The harsh taste of black licorice coated my mouth and throat and fought the anxiety in the pit of my body like Leonidas fighting off the Persians at the gates of Thermopylae.

It was a hopeless battle, but the Jager was putting up a hell of a fight.

The television was on and provided a minor soundtrack for the room. It kept playing ads for G*CTV, which I assumed was short for Griffin*Con Television. After a prolonged video of white text on black about a subject I didn't understand whatsoever, a man in a furry diaper and an axe was on the screen. He was speaking, but I could barely hear him. I doubt if I could understand what he was saying even if I could.

The fellow standing next to me was dressed in a white getup that reminded me of one of those *Star Wars* guys, but he wasn't wearing a helmet and had two white fanny packs on his sides. His legs were covered up with white, knee-high hooker boots. He had a black spandex coif that covered the top of his head, so he looked like a complete tool. He gave me the head cock, a sure sign that he wanted to talk to me.

"What's goin' on, man?"

It was obvious that the only two reasons he wanted to talk to me were because no one else was talking to him, and somehow he felt like I was the black sheep of the crowd. He was wearing a spandex coif and I was the fucking outcast.

"Nothing."

"You know Dave and Silvie?"

"Nope."

Bryan Young

"Oh." He took a swig of his bottled beer and stood in
awkward silence, looking at me expectantly, as though I was supposed to keep the conversation going.

"Nice costume."

"Oh, thanks. I've spent a lot of time on it." He looked
down around himself, taking in the sight of his own handiwork.

"What are you supposed to be, exactly?"

He sipped his beer and blinked. He must have thought I
was joking because he just grinned.

"Seriously."

"I'm a scout trooper from *Return of the Jedi.*"

"A scout trooper? Is that like one of those storm trooper
guys?"

"Yeah. But scout. I fly around on speeder bikes." He put
his mitts in the air and squatted slightly, flying through an imaginary landscape to illustrate his point.

"Oh."

"You've never seen *Return of the Jedi?*"

"Sure. Like twenty years ago."

"You haven't seen it since?"

"No. I don't go to the movies often. I'm a little surprised
it's as popular around here as it is."

"I think *Star Wars* being popular around here might be an
understatement."

"Really?"

"Yeah. I mean, I think the *Star Wars* fandom is the biggest
thing here. On top of all the book and movie tracks, you've got
the cartoon with a big presence. And as far as people, you've got

the 501st, the Rebel Legion, and the Mandalorian Mercs, and that's just the fan costume organizations alone."

"You one of those?"

"Am I one of..." He seemed truly flabbergasted and almost hurt. From one of his fanny packs he pulled a rank badge with his information etched into it clipped onto the lanyard. "TK-7451, Carolina Garrison. I've been in for eight years."

"And which one is that?"

"The 501st. Vader's fist? Ringing any bells?"

"So you guys get together and dress like the bad guys from an intergalactic civil war?"

"Yes, sir."

His patience with me was wearing thin and I could tell. He took a defiant sip from his bottle.

The moment I realized how seriously he took this was the moment I realized I could make this conversation a lot of fun.

"What makes that different than you guys getting together and dressing up like Nazis?"

It took a moment for that question to sink in. His brow furrowed and his free, black-gloved hand clenched into an angry fist. "What do you mean by that?"

"I mean really, aren't Vader's goons basically just the Nazis of *Star Wars*?"

"The difference is we never killed anybody."

"Did you guys blow up that whole planet? That's worse than anything Hitler ever did. Sure, he rounded up six million Jews and gassed them, but Vader ended the lives of what, six billion? And here you parade around and proudly wear the uniform?"

"Alderaan was fictional, you can't even begin to compare..."

"At the end of things, all we have are our stories. You and I don't know anybody affected by World War II, do we? Not personally. All we have are the stories, the cautionary tales. Sure, you may not believe in what the Imperials are espousing any more than you'd believe in what the Nazis did. But they both have a clear record and it speaks for itself. And the uniform that Stormtroopers or...well, I guess the Nazis called themselves that, too. Well, gray or white. It's all the same. "

"I really don't think you can compare the two."

"You might as well just have a big fucking swastika carved into your chestplate."

I looked him dead in the eyes while I chugged the rest of my beer.

"I think that's a little harsh, man. Do you have any idea how much charity work we do?"

Gulp. "Charity work?"

"I've worn this costume to hospitals all over the place, cheering sick kids up. My garrison has raised hundreds of thousands of dollars for charities. Sure, in the movies it's all about killing in white uniforms but out here in the real world we're all about giving back, helping people out."

I belched. "Maybe so."

Awash with incredulity, he cut his losses and simply walked away from me without another word.

Sure, maybe he was right and I was just a jackass. There was certainly more to all of this than I had guessed. And I would have never assumed that the guys who come to a convention like this would be so willing and capable to perform such incredible acts of public service.

I allowed myself a shrug and noticed that Katie, my beautiful, dark haired benefactor, was before me with a mooning grin.

"So, is this any better than the rest of what you've seen?"

"I dunno. Why are you so eager to please?"

"This place is magical and it makes me sad to think you're here all alone and hate it."

"Why do you care?"

She shrugged and her grin broadened. Her adorability was almost disgusting. "Who knows?"

Turning her back to me, she moved away with all the grace and confidence of a sex kitten. That sort of poise was rare and to be admired. If I had any admiration in my heart, I'm sure I'd care.

My heart didn't hold much but contempt for my fellow man these days. I was upset that didn't make me sad, but I got over it.

Across the room, Katie made her way to a fellow in slacks, black riding boots, and a long-sleeve tan shirt with gold trim. The pair of them spoke to each other conspiratorially. Something was afoot, but my suspicions weren't allowed enough time to fester properly, what with that tap on my shoulder.

It was Jessica. The blonde.

"Hey," she told me with a stupid grin.

"Hey back."

She was dancing in place with a pair of beer bottles. She offered me one, so I took it and popped its top. Then, with the bottle, I indicated Katie and her costumed friend.

"Who's that guy?"

"The Captain?"

"I guess so."

"He's The Captain."

"That's his name?"

"I don't know his name, but he's dressed as a Captain."

"Is that so?"

"Yup."

"She interested in him?"

I could understand if he was. He was young and had a wide, dimpled smile. And you could barely see the girdle under his uniform.

Jessica giggled. "No. He's our hook up."

"Is that so?"

"Is that all you do? Ask questions and say, 'Is that so?'"

"I'm a journalist. It's my job to ask the hard questions."

"Is that so?" She suppressed a giggle.

"That's the long and the short of it."

"So, you want in on this?"

"On what?"

"On this."

Jessica drew my attention to the dance between Katie and her Captain. Casually, Katie passed The Captain a wad of folded bills and he passed her a small bag of indeterminate contents.

"Probably."

"Wanna chip in?"

And so their cards were on the table. I looked like someone who would help spread the cost of their habit. And the whole point of coming up here was meeting up with this guy, I'm sure.

"Fuck it."

"No then?"

"Did I say that?"

I took a random bill from my back pocket and, like the asshole I am, tucked it neatly into Jessica's exposed cleavage.

For some reason this was not offensive to her. On the contrary, this served as cause for a hearty chuckle. She fished what turned out to be a twenty-dollar bill from between her perky breasts. They'd been quite firm and wonderful. I couldn't remember the last time I'd touched a breast and had a reaction like that.

Jesus.

I could do no wrong with these girls. What had I done to be offered such a ridiculously valuable blank check?

Being nice certainly wasn't it.

Katie motioned with her head that we should follow her and we made our slow egress back toward the front of the room. Around and over people we stepped, carefully.

As we passed The Captain, I nodded to him respectfully, "Captain."

"Ensign." He nodded back.

The girls led me into the bathroom and closed the door behind us, locking it.

Katie poured the contents out on the counter and it was a white powder, cocaine was my guess. My contribution to the haul probably wasn't enough to make a dent in the purchase they just made, but at least it was a nice gesture.

Shut up.

I am too capable of nice gestures now and again.

Cocaine wasn't usually my thing. To be honest, I didn't like it all that much, it made me a raving madman, but I was past the point of caring.

Katie quite competently divided the white powder into three even lines while Jessica quite stereotypically rolled up the twenty-dollar bill I'd stuffed into her bra.

Jessica offered me the bill and the first turn, which I gladly accepted.

Snort, snort, snort.

The acetone bitterness I was expecting was replaced with something more chemical. I could feel it dripping through my nasal cavity down the back of my throat and I panicked. What could this new substance be?

What would these adorable young girls be snorting?

"What is this?" I asked as I passed the dollar bill to Katie.

Jessica answered, "Aunt Molly."

"Who the fuck is Aunt Molly?"

"It's X."

"X?"

"Ecstasy. You've never done ecstasy before?"

"No. I'm not a twelve year old girl."

"You'll love it."

"How long have I got?"

"Ten, maybe twenty minutes."

Katie inhaled two breaths worth of air in through her nostrils and handed Jessica the cash.

So what if I'd never tried this stuff? I think that makes me more of a man, not less.

"What's the score here? What happens next?"

"We have a great time is what happens."

"Where to?"

"There's a dance floor downstairs that's perfect for this."

I cracked open the bathroom door, making sure the coast was clear and that's when my jaw dropped. There in the doorway, drinking a beer, was the immortal Mr. Lincoln. He was engaged deeply in a conversation, most likely about matters of national importance, including, but not limited to, the assassination of enemies of state. I could only imagine that I was one of these enemies that needed removing. How else could I explain the ubiquity of this man?

He must have been following me.

Forcefully, I shut the door and turned back to the girls.

"What's wrong?" One of them asked, I didn't see which.

"Nothing."

"Then why did you slam the door?"

"It's just..." Did I dare tell them about my paranoia? Was I even being paranoid? Space Lincoln was appearing everywhere I went. Each time he appeared he'd been more and more menacing. If he were to see me again, I could only imagine that his glowering might burn a hole through me.

"Just what?"

"Is there something out there, Cobb?"

"Yes."

"What's out there?"

"The sixteenth President of the United States is out there. He's been brought back from the dead with cybernetic enhancements. I told him my name was Jefferson Davis and I'm pretty sure he's trying to kill me for it."

Predictably, they giggled uncontrollably.

"I'm not kidding."

They offered to shield me from his view if I was so worried about it and I accepted immediately.

Jessica left the bathroom first, then me, finally Katie took up the rear and closed the bathroom door delicately behind her. Lincoln had his back turned to us and, by tiptoeing quietly by him, I'd hoped that we'd avoid his gaze completely.

With any luck, he'd never even know I was there. Unless he already knew I was there and that's why he came. I could never be sure. He'd been a crafty one throughout his entire political career.

Jessica opened the door, stepped out, and held it open for me. I turned back, trying to ensure that the former President hadn't spotted me, but it was not meant to be. Our eyes locked and he grinned his big Lincoln grin like a cat who'd soon be eating the canary.

"Jeff," Lincoln said in his rich baritone, taking me completely by surprise.

"Shit!"

Shooting right past Jessica, I sprinted out of the room and ran as far down the hallway as I could before I realized I was completely lost.

Every floor was identical all the way around and my head was spinning as it was. I was intoxicated and being pursued by the most sinister and effective agent our country ever had the fiendish desire to muster. Getting lost was an exercise in inevitability.

Winded, I collapsed to the floor, hoping that by remaining as close to the ground as possible I'd avoid the tall gaze of Lincoln. I'm positive I was muttering to myself there on the floor when the girls found me.

Their giggling had matured into deep and hearty laughter.

Katie and Jessica reached down and pulled me up off the ground, chortling the whole time. They managed to stifle their laughter while I dusted myself off.

Doing my hardest to look as though nothing ridiculous had just happened, I sighed. "So. What's the score here?"

They tee-heed violently, like high pitched motorcycle engines. If it were up to me to guess, I'd have assumed this was the funniest thing their adorable little faces had ever seen.

Fuck me.

"Now it's time for the party."

"Where's the party?"

Katie pointed down over the balcony into the madness of the lobby of the Marriott. At this point, calling it merely a lobby seemed disingenuous. It was more than a lobby. This was the center of the party, the very heart of it.

It was like the fiery steam engine at the heart of a barreling locomotive. It was the coal-fired centrifuge that spun off at a thousand miles an hour, launching people down every hallway shaped artery connected to it. It was a people furnace and it burned us all up like fuel. If we weren't careful it would smoke us all down to the filter.

Bryan Young

The worst part about it was that it was completely out of control. It was a circus. A carnival. A Ringling Brothers and Barnum and Bailey extravaganza.

The costumes had grown more fanciful, the booze more potent, the crowd ballooned to twice its previous numbers.

It was then, walking around on the outskirts of this mess with the girls, that I noticed that a spot had opened in my soul. It was like my innards and emotions had been completely closed off to light and an aperture had opened up, letting the dark and the stress and the evil out from deep inside me. Just like a camera, the aperture let in the light and goodness and enjoyment I never knew I was capable of.

I sucked down hard on the bottle of my beer and it felt amazing. I could feel the cold glass rim on my lips and it tingled and vibrated down the core of my existence. The brew entered into my throat and trickled lovingly down into my gullet.

Somehow, every sensation that had become commonplace to me had been amplified and magnified to the point of ecstasy.

Oh.

Right.

The ecstasy.

Shit.

Between the alcohol and the ecstasy, I couldn't be sure if this would create some sort of bizarre push-pull effect or if the combination of the two would create a brand new feeling that would take me to heights never before imagined in my life.

Katie and Jessica, the two most caring and adoring girls in my universe, took me by the hands and we floated down, down,

down into the heart of the people furnace and then we skimmed around the edges toward our pending revelry.

I could see us in the third person, skipping along; a pathway magically opened up among the crowd, like the Red Sea when Charlton Heston parted it in the Bible. Or the Yellow Brick Road. We came to a ballroom attached to the celebratory centrifuge and waited in line to enter.

That's when I could feel the reality slipping from me. I knew that ecstasy wasn't necessarily hallucinogenic, but I've always been far too open to visions and seeing things. When I was a kid, I had a hard time discerning reality from fantasy and I'd had a horde of imaginary friends. My favorite of these friends was a kid named Dave. Sadly, Dave and I had a bit of a falling out when I was eleven. It wasn't a very pleasant experience for me.

I was actually pretty devastated.

He left me forever after we argued about the real name of John Wayne. He didn't believe me that he was really a bigoted ultraconservative named Marion Morrison. Even though Dave turned out to be a pretty stupid bastard, I'm not sure I ever really got over the loss.

Before I knew it, we were inside the party. I'm not sure how we got in: the girls had led me by the hand and before I could blink we were in.

The throbbing beat of the dance music from inside the ballroom was hypnotizing, but not as much as the deep blue strobe light that was blinking on and off in time with the music. Katie was dragging me into the darkness and I could feel her soft, delicate hand in mine.

As our skin brushed together, it felt as if I could feel deep down into her very soul. It felt like our hearts almost touched, but not quite. They were close enough for the spark of consciousness and life to arc between us, though, just like in Michelangelo's *Creation of Adam* in the midst of the Sistine Chapel.

The stress and hate in my heart began to melt like an ice cube under a heat lamp, but I wanted to keep it and hold on to it somehow. That derision in my heart was the only comforting constant in my life and it was slipping away from me like sands through an hourglass.

I couldn't let that stand, but I was powerless to do anything about it.

We passed by the fringe of the dance party, right by the wallflowers. One was literally dressed like a flower. I wanted to pluck her and present her to Katie, which was in itself a bizarre experience. For one, I'd never felt the urge to give a woman a flower in my life, and for two, I wasn't interested in Katie even in the slightest. Nor was I interested in Jessica for that matter. They were dazzling on the eyes, sure, but I yearned for Laurie.

My Laurie.

The clever girl that she was, Katie brought me directly to the bar for a libation. The next step I took was onto a thick, white shag carpet. A blast of cold air from somewhere or another hit me and I got the distinct feeling I was in an igloo. And I simply couldn't take my eyes off of the ice sculptures that were on display around the bar. Bright blue lights were aimed directly at the statuary, giving each of the sculptures the impression that they were much colder than they were. They were sweating and losing their shape, giving them an eerie look. A thick fog rolled through, sticking low and close to the ground.

For one shivering moment the illusion was complete and I really felt as though I were in an ice-cave. The cold air blowing through the area felt like a breath of minty fresh air on my skin. It was so refreshing that I felt like a completely new person.

Altered states were never my forte.

I could feel myself feeling fine and it reminded me with no malice why my drug of choice was alcohol. I could perpetuate my self-loathing without having to think about it. In this state I'd have to try to hate me.

But I couldn't.

The most unnerving thing about this sensation was that I felt as though I was high up on a trapeze platform without a safety net. I was in unsafe territory, high above the earth, and the only thing between the ground and me was air and imminent death.

I thought things were bad, but they took a turn for the worse with the appearance of a massive rodent.

I've never been afraid of mice, but it was startling to me that there was a giant yellow mouse standing next me, giving hugs to all comers.

The mouse was easily six-foot-five and had a bright and smiling head four times larger than my own, situated beneath a green bowler. His face was contorted into a vast, permanent grin with bright white teeth that were a harsh purple under the nearby black light. Its body seemed to be nothing more than a yellow, fleece nightgown that met a pair of giant yellow feet. He wore a green necktie to match his bowler.

To my horror, not only did I find myself compelled to embrace this overgrown vermin, I found myself actually doing it. Worse than that? It wasn't so bad.

The fleece of his body was soft against my skin and warm and comforting. I had a fleeting moment of panic when I couldn't tell the gender of the mouse, but I realized it didn't matter. It didn't care if I was some drunk, stupid bastard; it just wanted to hug me because I was a person.

Much could be learned from this mouse.

I didn't want to let this rodent out of my sight. Being a man didn't matter so much anymore if being a mouse was so much more rewarding.

"Katie," I shouted over the music, looking for my companion. She was at the bar, ordering a drink. Her eyes met mine and she smiled, showing me that she'd bought me a drink, too. Clever girl.

"You have to hug this mouse, man. This is fucking incredible."

She handed me my beverage and I insisted that she took a turn hugging the oversized rodent.

She pulled away, but couldn't take her hands off of his fleece arms and mittens. "Would you join us for a drink, Mister Mouse?"

It nodded its head up and down enthusiastically and covered its mouth with both hands as though it were suppressing a laugh.

Jesus this thing was adorable. Why didn't they have mice like this back home?

Katie led the chain of us, with the mouse in the middle, toward a table in the back of the room where we sat and set out a sort of tea party with our booze.

I wondered if we needed to fetch some cheese for our new friend. Then I spent a minute trying to figure out if I'd said that out loud or simply thought it. Then I realized it didn't matter, because even if I did say it out loud, I would have muttered it and no one would have been able to hear it beneath the crushing weight of the dance music.

As soon as we were situated, I thought I'd ask more force-fully. "Do we need to fetch you some cheese?"

It pantomimed as though it couldn't hear me.

"Do you need some fucking cheese, man?"

My guess is that everyone could hear that. It felt as though a record had scratched and the party stopped. All eyes in our general vicinity came on to me as though I'd screamed some-thing offensive at the top of my lungs.

Why were they all looking at me?

For Christ's sake, make it stop!

The mouse once again pantomimed his laugh. Somehow that made it all better for the crowd. They all went about their business and the party continued. Now we could get on with our tea party.

"We need some cakes for this tea. Where's Jesse? She should be here with our cakes."

"Jessica? She's over there." Katie pointed to a girl on the dance floor bumping and grinding into another female specimen. She was so sexual a creature I almost didn't recognize her. She was rubbing her ass into the vagina of a girl of a metal bikini. It

115

seemed as though the girl in the metal bikini had a chain around her throat that Jessica had pulled up over her shoulder.

One of the wallflowers shouted at Jessica, "Show us your boobs!"

Jessica dropped her captive's chain and grabbed the bottom of her skirt, pulling up on it to show her white cotton panties and black lace bra that barely contained the soft, lovely flesh beneath them.

Do I really need to tell you I was aroused?

Who wouldn't be? They were hot.

I sipped my tea. The liquid hit my tongue and took me off guard. Instead of a smooth herbal tea, there was the sharp taste like furniture polish or booze in my mouth, trickling down my throat. "My tea's been spiked. What about yours?"

"No one's spiked your tea!"

The mouse laughed again.

The room was spinning and they were all laughing at me again.

"I'd like to get off, please."

"What?"

"I'd like to get off."

"Get off what?"

It was then that I stood and ambled away from our tea party. The mouse could go fuck himself and so could the girl. Kristen?

Step after careful step, I made my way to the dance floor where Jesse and the masochism girl were dancing with each other and tried getting in between them. I think I might have grabbed an ass. Or a breast. Maybe one with each hand.

"What the fuck?"

My cheek was stinging from a slap, so I left before they caused an even bigger scene.

I had to get out of the dancing room place, but everything was so blue and it all looked the same. Faces passed by me as though I were looking out from inside a fishbowl.

Stumbling to the floor, I noticed that I'd tripped on a cape that looked purple in the azure light and I grabbed at it, hoping that it was connected to something sturdy enough to hold my weight.

The owner of the cape, attuned to my tugging, turned and picked me up by the scruff of my neck. When my feet were firmly planted I thanked the man who came to my aid.

He wasn't any man. He was a super man. He was *the* Superman. And he wasn't a shabby Superman, either. But he was pissed. This was like *Superman III* Superman. This brute had a day of stubble and everything. And I'd tugged on his fucking cape.

"What the fuck, mate?" He was asking me.

I muttered a string of nonsense, hoping he'd let me just carry on. He wasn't in his right mind, though.

"Didn't anybody tell you, you never tug on Superman's cape?"

Oh, Jesus. He'd noticed.

I did more babbling. Since I couldn't be sure what I was saying, I was positive he wasn't sure either.

"Jog on, fucker."

He gave me a good shove into the crowd and picked his dance steps back up where he'd left off before I interrupted him.

Petrified, I didn't know what to do. Did I shake it off and walk away? Or did I challenge the Man of Steel for being a dick and completely out of character?

I'm going to be honest: this was never a situation I ever thought I'd be in.

As my mind processed all of my options and information, it turns out my body, and possibly the drugs, decided my course of action for me. My arms were around Superman, embracing him and sobbing like a damned fool.

"It's okay, man. It's all okay. I'm sorry I tugged on your cape."

"Get the fuck off me."

"It's okay, I'm so sorry."

All I wanted to do was let him know that it was all okay, which is why I couldn't understand the need for my face and his fists to become as well acquainted as they did. All it took was one stiff punch in my mouth and I let go, deciding I'd leave him be. I really couldn't blame him at all. What happens if Metropolis were in trouble and he was too busy dealing with me? It was my duty-- no, my honor--to let him go and carry on my way, looking for the exit from this magical place. A split lip was a small price to pay.

Faltering was all I was capable of, so I faltered away toward the walls. If I found an edge to this disco ice cavern I'm sure I'd somehow find a portal out.

A white light in the distance amid the sea of blue drew me toward it, like a moth to the flame. Sadly, the wallflowers stood between me and the pearly gates of egress.

Putting a hand on each one, I counted each of them as I ambled forward, step by step. One, two, three, four, was that a girl's ass I just touched?

Five, six, that was definitely a breast.

Another shove to my back, so I had to skip a couple of them, ten, eleven, twelve. Did someone just smack my ass with a sword?

Fourteen. Fifteen.

I had made it as close as three people away from the sallow light of the exit when a gorilla stood in my way. It wasn't a metaphorical gorilla, either. It was an actual, living, breathing gorilla with a white collar and a black bowtie around his neck. His wrists were adorned with matching white cuffs and in his left hand he held a pistol with all the arrogance of a secret agent. It was sleek and black and the silencer had a soft reflection of the sapphire light across its length, giving it shape in the dark.

I froze. Had someone freed this poor creature from a nearby zoo and dressed him up for some sick fantasy? What were they up to?

Terror was the only word that could describe my demeanor. I'd seen far too many documentaries on the nature channels to know that he could break me in two without a second thought. Worse than that, he had a gun!

Hoping he didn't notice me, I tried to tiptoe around him, which was a difficult task since the high tide of dancers had ebbed up into this area.

The ape stood upright and looked around, looking for me, obviously. I covered my eyes with my hands like a frightened child.

Bryan Young

Peeking from between my fingers, I carried on in my slow arc around him, hoping I could make it out with my life intact.

That's when his eyes locked with mine.

I panicked. "Don't kill me. I welcome death, but this isn't the way I saw things ending, man. I just want out."

His face recoiled in confusion. Somehow he understood me?

He raised his meaty paw up, gun in hand, and pointed to the door.

Was he offering me safe passage? Or wanting to just shoot me in the back?

I couldn't tell, but I'd take my chances. I dove for the door and made it out with a neat tuck and roll, letting the fresh lobby air fill my lungs.

I'd gone out of the proverbial frying pan and into the fryer. Though the light was better and the music wasn't jamming the signals in my brain and throbbing into my bloodstream, there were easily a hundred fold more people here.

And then something ran into my foot.

You know that little domey robot from *Star Wars*? He was there, ramming into my legs. But instead of silver and blue he was colored black and yellow. He kept whistling at me and running into my leg like a dog in heat.

"What the fuck is this new devilry?"

He beeped and chortled more. The little guy clearly had something to say, but I couldn't understand him. We didn't speak the same language.

"What are you saying?"

This fucking thing shrieked a whistle at me. His message must have been important.

"I don't understand you, man. You have something for me?"

With a spark and a pop, something on the top of the robot exploded, smoke was everywhere. It squawked hideously and I could hear a voice saying something that made little sense about a bad motivator. It startled me so badly I was bowled over from my haunches to my ass. From the corner of my eye, I could see an overweight fellow in a black uniform with a tight cap laughing hysterically with his hands behind his back.

I tried to ignore him and carried on. "Are you okay little guy?"

The robot swung his top dome back and forth, almost as if to tell me no. If only he and I had a means of communication we could sort this out, but that fucking guy kept laughing at us.

Before I knew it I was in this guy's face. "What, sir, is your fucking problem?"

He could barely form words through the laughter in his mouth and the tears in his eyes. His ample paunch convulsed up and down with each belly laugh.

"What's so goddamned funny?"

He wheezed and hissed, trying hard to stop his merriment, but he only backed up and produced his hands from behind his back. In them was a remote control device one would expect you'd see operating a radio controlled car or model airplane. "It's the..."

"It's the what?"

I was completely incensed. I didn't take kindly to people laughing at me and this poor little robot needed my help. It was wounded, hurt real bad, and this guy was just laughing at us.

"It's the..." He couldn't finish his sentence. He just broke down, hunched over in tears.

"It's the what? Out with it, man! Speak the fuck up!"

After gasping for a breath, just this close to hyperventilating, he was able to eek out a few words, "The droid... It's the droid..."

That's when it clicked. He was the puppet master.

How could I be so stupid?

Of course the robot wasn't real. The controller. He was controlling it.

Heat was rising in my cheeks and I could tell that I was blushing from mortified embarrassment. There was a snapping of fingers in my brain.

Fuck.

Damn it all to hell. It was the drugs. I realized I was under the horrible spell of the drugs and they were making me act like a fucking crazy person.

I had to get out of here.

How would I maintain any of my journalistic integrity if I was down here on the floor in front of my subjects and potential readers raving like a lunatic?

I had to think fast.

How would I get out of this mess?

To make matters worse, I hadn't noticed that I'd clenched this stupid, stupid fat man's uniform up at the chest and I was bearing my teeth at him like a caged animal.

Letting go of fistfuls of cloth, I smoothed the wrinkles out of his shirt and closed my mouth. Conscious of the scowl I'd been sporting, I made an effort to calm my features and appear stoic in the face of such adversity.

"I'm sorry. It was...uh...it was my mistake. That's all it was. A simple mistake. I was...uh...I was kidding. Yeah, that's the ticket."

Finally, his laughter subsided and he backed away from me. I was unnervingly close to him and obviously a crazy person so I couldn't blame him for backing up.

"Run!"

That's what my mind told me to do. That's what I said out loud, apparently, and that's what I did. I turned and ran headfirst into the crowd, hoping that he'd lose me in the milieu.

With any luck, I'd never see that fat bastard and his robot ever again.

Now the problem was making it to the elevators.

Holy hell.

Navigating this place, even in a straight line of sight from one side of the room to other, was a challenge. Not just a challenge. It was a Herculean task, and, like Hercules, I'd be more than happy to kill my wife and child to get through this mess and just be in my bed sleeping and claim temporary insanity afterwards.

I'm not sure why, but it hurt me to think that I couldn't recognize at least ninety percent of the costumes I passed by. In my field, I'm used to being able to recognize even the most obscure politicians by sight. I could tell you the name of the last three Agriculture Secretaries and the giant food manufacturers they worked for before and after their tenure, but in this place I was barely keeping up.

I was the guy people nudged and asked questions to when they didn't know what was what and I was suddenly thrust into a world I hadn't known anything about since the ninth grade.

It was unsettling.

That's when I noticed Laurie standing across the room. She was dressed as some manner of elf in metal armour that covered little more than her naughty bits. Was that Laurie? It couldn't be, but somehow it was. Why would my mind do that? It was probably because there was a physically imposing and inarguably attractive barbarian kissing her neck and back from behind. Not-Laurie was thrilled and clearly enjoying his meaty advances. He navigated his lips around her long black hair and pointy ears, brushing her skin lightly. She shuddered with delight.

Jealousy boiled within me.

When she turned around and I could take into account her hourglass shape and bare back, I was smitten. She was shaped identically to Laurie and it caused a swelling in my loins. Laurie's avatar kissed the barbarian and the swelling boiled over and my jealousy hit the flames beneath the pot and I knew I had to keep moving but was powerless to continue.

She wrapped her bare leg around the barbarian and he gyrated his hips into her.

Kissing his chest, she whispered into his ear. A smile crept across his face and they both looked around, leaving their public space. Presumably they left in search of somewhere more private where he could impale her with his sword. Or penis. Either one. Probably both.

My heart sank, killing the warmth of the drugs. The urge for locomotion finally returned to my legs and I continued my excursion to the elevator.

That feeling of flying high without a safety net returned as the elevator doors I'd finally reached opened with a sharp DING.

And there before me was Darth Vader, or at least some impostor playing him.

He was all in black, save the lights twinkling on his chest plate. He had his laser sword swinging at his side and a boom box straight out of 1985 slung on his shoulder.

Jesus Christ almighty, I was in hell.

Run DMC was blaring, but Vader, with a thick, gloved hand, pressed pause on the tape player ceasing the music. All was silent but for his asthmatic voice, "Party Vader 'Vater."

I had no idea what he said, but what else could I do? I stepped into the elevator with this evil man and his entourage, dressed in costumes from half a different film fantasies. Squeezing into the back, I thought I'd just zone them out, staring out at the floors below.

When the elevator doors closed, Vader once more resumed his assault on decency, filling the airwaves with the mingent sounds of early eighties hip-hop. The rest joined in on the merriment and it was as though I'd stepped into a cage for a dozen go-go dancers.

We made it up five floors before the doors opened and I wanted to scream out to those getting on, "Run! Flee for your insignificant lives!"

Before I could utter a syllable, Vader beat me to the punch. "Party Vader 'Vater," he would say, just after stopping the music. I rolled those words back and forth in my head trying to make sense of them to no avail.

The doors closed, he restarted the music, and the dance party began all over again.

By the time we finally reached the ninth floor, it was apparent to me that my heart might explode. When the door opened I was clamoring to get out, but there was an entire boarding party of people standing in my way, expecting to get on.

They were all dressed in khaki jumpsuits, each of them had hexagonal white patches with rows of solid black lines embroidered along the inside.

It was a shock to everyone, me most of all, when I shoved the Vader down to his knees, all while I was screaming like a madman. "Get out! Run for your lives! Get out while you still can!"

I made it out and hit the front most khaki clad bastard with my shoulder and it was as though I'd struck their tenpin. They all toppled over, sprawling across the floor.

That's when I felt a chill coarse through my blood, starting at my heart and stopping me in my tracks.

He was there.

Looking at me, staring at the commotion I'd caused.

Who else but Abraham Lincoln?

He was coming out of a room some thirty feet away and with all of my hollering he had to notice me. His copper-plated goggles whirred into focus, almost certainly narrowing in on me. I wondered if his eyewear contained some sort of heads up display that had targeted me, painting a giant bulls eye on my forehead.

I didn't have much time to count the different ways he could crush me with his augmented hands because I was already on my way back into the elevator. Clawing my way inside, I prayed his stovepipe hat wasn't brimmed with a steel blade, perfect for throwing like a discus and beheading me like some half-assed Bond villain from the sixties.

The Vader turned to me and, in his belabored voice, asked me, "What the fuck?"

Ignoring him, I made my way to the back of the elevator, hurrying my way past the dancers. I went as far as I could and hit a glass wall, looking out over the lobby and turned to see if the steam powered Lincoln was still on my trail.

Lincoln seemed to have forgotten about me. He was using his meaty bionic arms to help up the guys dressed like janitors that I'd knocked over like brick houses in a hurricane.

Our eyes locked, Lincoln's and mine. This was a battle of titans and I was determined to stay as far away from the battlefield as possible. Our eyes remained fixed until the doors slid shut and the dance party continued upwards.

The rap hits of the eighties began again and the walls shook from the shifting weight of the merrymakers.

The elevator shot upwards.

As I watched the dots on the floor below get smaller and smaller, I was left in my own thoughts, considering the ever-expanding nature of the universe. My brain hurt contemplating the idea that telescopes in space could see the edge of the big bang and that seeing light at immense distances was tantamount to time travel. Perceiving the vastness of the universe while rising higher and higher into the upper bowels of the hotel made my head swim.

The intoxicating effects of the methylenedioxymetham-phetamine in my system were only exacerbating the ethereal pain throbbing in my head. The people in the lobby below were shrinking, getting smaller and smaller, their lives more and more insignificant. They were just like me. Even though I was moving higher and higher, I was matching their insectoid size, contracting into my own original fetal state. The galaxy was drifting further and further into the far reaches of space and our space telescopes were looking deeper and deeper into the depths of time and I could feel that swirl of emotional discomfort, like that first walk into a strange girl's bedroom.

There in the void was the head of Lincoln, floating in the ectoplasm of the universe. His mouth opened and consumed my small, floating, infantile form until I was what Vonnegut would call a wisp of undifferentiated nothingness.

There was blackness.

And then after the blackness, there was nothing.

Part Two: Embedded

GRIFFIN*CON: THE "NERDY-GRAS" OF GEEK DEBAUCHERY
By M. Cobb

Atlanta, GA - Sex, Drugs, Rock and Roll. Not often are these things associated with the base-ment dwelling denizens of Geekdom. Most of the costumed women are attractive and inviting and most of the costumed men defy stereotype.

Much like the Mardis Gras of New Orleans, the nightlife of Griffin*Con is a fanciful affair with costumes and streamers, music and food, and plenty of drugs and booze. "Show me your boobs!" was a war cry heard often, and just as often was that plea acted upon. Impressionable young girls dressed in costumes ranging from students in the Harry Potter Universe to the elves of Middle Earth pulled up their shirts and skirts to oblige the horny masses of Griffin*Con.

Though this all seems like a very good time, it is easy to wonder if this behavior is healthy amongst a niche of people known for their lim-ited contact with the outside world.

Drugs like cocaine, ecstasy, marijuana, and more alcohol than can be quantified all have a pres-ence at Griffin*Con (arguably those drugs have a presence everywhere in society), but does that make this a family affair? If you plan to travel to Griffin*Con in the future, think long and hard about bringing the wife and kids.

I

"Thanks for letting me crash on your floor. I didn't want to bug you while you were sleeping, but thanks again."

That soft voice was the sound that woke me up, presumably the next morning. I was confident that it was Saturday, but anything was possible.

I never knew the name of the girl, but through cracked eyelids I could see that she was a slightly chunky, mildly attractive cosplayer wearing a revealing red dress, red stilettos, and a platinum blonde wig.

I was terrified she was a hooker.

That initial, terrible thought was what motivated me to get up out of bed. Ordinarily that depressed feeling I was experiencing would keep me in bed for as long as possible.

She was out the door and gone before I could ask her what happened. A cursory inspection of my wallet revealed that I wasn't missing any serious amounts of cash. Add that to the fact that she'd slept at the foot of the bed beneath the comforter probably equaled that she wasn't a hooker.

That, and a whore would have slept in the bed with me. Or maybe she wouldn't have.

Shit.

I didn't know.

There was a gnawing hatred in my heart. Hatred for myself. Hatred for my job. Hatred for my failed relationship. Hatred for the universe.

I tried not to think about all that and just wrote up something about the night before and sent it off. I wrote it up, pulling details from the air like clouds of cotton candy. None of it was good for me and it would make my teeth rot out, but it did the job it was supposed to.

I don't even know what I'm saying anymore.

Is any of this really happening to me?

I needed something else. I needed to find something about this entire event that gave me some redeeming hope for the continuation of our species. Because at this point, sure there were some cute girls, and some of the vague and foggy parts of the night previous had moments of fun or elation to them, but this entire enterprise was an abortion in the grand scheme of human drama.

My intense desire to be an agoraphobic tugged at the edges of my reason, but I had to find something out there.

I had to.

With that concrete resolve in my heart, I made it all the way to the gift shop in the lobby without suffering any serious form of panic attack. I'm guessing that at least part of that was because I knew I was leaving my room to buy a fifth of scotch from the gift shop and had a destination in mind outside of the hotel.

Destination: Fresh air outside of this dive.

On my way out of the hotel I sipped straight from the fifth of Glen like a baby nursing on a bottle. When I arrived in Atlanta, there was never a moment I thought I'd feel safe enough in this rat's nest of a city to find sitting on the curb and drinking scotch from the bottle as something relaxing.

Maybe it was me I hated more than Atlanta. Atlanta didn't seem so bad. I just hated where I was because I was there.

There was no place I could go to get far enough away without getting lost, so I was stuck sitting right outside the Marriott, just beyond the overhang of the valet's roundabout, staring at the ass end of another hotel. There was a black marble planter on the street and it seems like as good a place as any to get drunk.

At the hotel across the street was a line of people that began at a glass door and stretched down to the sidewalk and around the corner.

They were waiting for something. I admired their enthusiasm.

As I sat there, considering the fate of man in the context of the expanding universe, I realized that at least part of my depression could be attributed to the drugs I'd consumed the night before. I'd released what little dopamine I had scraped together in my brain for the chemical effects and now I was afflicted with having none, making me feel like shit. The rest of my depression could be attributed to my shitty station in life. I'd have to take responsibility for that.

Part of taking responsibility for that would be harder than it sounded. It was difficult because it would involve admitting that the problem was rooted in decisions I'd made for myself.

And sometimes that process is nigh on impossible.

"Hey, man. Whatchoo doin' out here?"

"Huh?" What the fuck was this treachery?

Someone placed a hand squarely on my back in a disgusting, familiar way. I panicked, praying that Space Lincoln hadn't caught up to me. If he had, what would he do to me? He freed the slaves and sewed the country back together, he was capable of anything and could snap me like a twig.

To my eternal relief, I turned to see it was Sylvester, the homeless man, taking a seat next to me. He seemed to be without a care in the world.

"Uh...." I was stunned, though it should have been no surprise to me that the one human being I showed a genuine act of kindness to would seek me out.

"The party's all up in there, man. Whatchoo doin' out here?"

I wondered if he was a con man, not homeless at all, just back here for more; ready to spend my hard earned cash on some bit of useless crap available inside.

But he was wearing the same clothes he'd worn when I encountered him before. By the smell of him, I'd guess they were the same clothes he'd been wearing all week. Maybe longer.

The smell coming off of him was somewhere between an unwashed pair of underwear after a week of camping and a dumpster.

Meh. Fuck it.

I shrugged in response and offered him the bottle of scotch I'd been nursing like a breast.

"No thanks, man. I can't afford to touch the stuff. I 'preciate the gesture, though."

"It's a god damn circus in there, Sylvester. But what are you doing out here?"

"Shit, man. You remembered my name? You know me, I got nowhere else to be. And like I said, this is where the party is. All the people are around, I figure maybe what little I can do for 'em might make me enough to eat tonight. Thanks to you, though, I been eatin' good all day."

"I helped that much?"

"You kidding? It meant the world to me."

"Let me ask you this, Sylvester, what did you do before living like this?"

"I worked construction. Got downsized out of the company, housing market collapsed. I know I'm not too bright, no college or nothin', barely any high school. But I can build the shit out of shit, know what I'm sayin'? People ain't buildin' shit these days. Else it all gets foreclosed on."

"Didn't you get unemployment?"

"Spent a year on unemployment."

"What about all this geek stuff. You seem to know all about the con. You any good with it?"

"Shit, yeah, man. I used to read Superman comics every week like clockwork until I lost my job. Superman's the shit. I even dressed up like Steel one time for this thing."

"Steel?"

"You don't know John Henry Irons, man? He's the black Superman. He's got a sledgehammer, even took over for Superman for a while when he died."

"Superman died?"

"Yeah, back twenty years ago when guys like us were in high school."

"That was after my time." I was feigning a bit of ignorance on this one, and for that I was sorry. I knew Superman had died. I had to write a story about it on the politics beat because Clinton spoke at the funeral.

"Yeah, those were good times. Everybody needs it, you know? Superheroes give guys like us somethin' to look up to. Ain't nothin' else to look up to no more. At least in comics they still do right because it's the right thing to do. Not like out here. Not like out here at all."

Strong stuff.

"You any good with a camera?"

"Huh?"

"You can run a camera, right? Take pictures?"

"I guess so. Where you goin' with this, man?"

"What if I hired you to be my photographer for today? I haven't taken a single picture. I'll get you a credential and my camera and you just go to town."

"Shit, man."

"I'll pay you a hundred bucks."

"A hundred bucks?"

"A hundred bucks."

How could I be sure he wouldn't just get the camera and the money and run off with it? The thought crossed my mind, but I simply filled myself with ambivalence like a hot air balloon until I could feel my doubts floating away. Even if he did abscond with the funds and the camera, what was it to me? I'd just tell the editor I got mugged.

Hell, that could be a story right there.

"You not fuckin' wit' me?"

"Why would I fuck with you? You've been fucked with long enough. But you seem to know your way around and as long as you can snap pictures with a robot camera that does everything for you, why not? I don't want to be bothered with it and you need the money."

Sylvester's face broadened into a wide, toothy grin. "Then I'm your man, dude."

"I only wish I could offer you more money." It was true. I wasn't bullshitting that part. I wish I could have given him something more. A hundred bucks wasn't going to put this man back on his feet but it would go a long way to help him out in the short term. For the life of me, I couldn't decide why it seemed to matter, but whatever.

I guess everybody has a kind streak to them.

Except maybe lobbyists.

Fuck those guys.

After an hour of meandering my way through hallways and up and down escalators across three hotels, I found my way back to the media room to get Sylvester a press pass. The guy there was hesitant, but he really didn't have a choice, so he relented.

Another hour would have been spent finding my hotel room, but Sylvester knew exactly the way back. I let him shower in my room, gave him some of my clothes, and handed him my camera and a hundred bucks.

"What is it you want me takin' pictures of exactly?"

"Anything. Panels. Celebrities. Hot chicks in costumes."

As I said that last bit, I had a vision of the night previous but I couldn't tell if it was from a dream or a drug-induced revelation. The image was that of two girls, one was in chains and a bikini, the other in the short dress of a schoolgirl. They were sucking on each other.

"Yeah. I think that did happen."

"What?"

"Nothing. Nothing. Just fill up the camera."

"You're the shit, man. You won't regret this."

"I better not."

"You won't."

"Let's just get the fuck to it, yes? We don't have all day to stand here and talk. We need to find a fucking story."

"Sure thing, man."

There was a snap and a sharp flash in my eyes. I was Raymond Burr in Jimmy Stewart's apartment, blinded. Perhaps not permanently, but blinded nonetheless. The daffy bastard had snapped a photo of me. The edges of my vision faded from white to red and back to a monochromatic version of the real world.

"So, what's the first story?"

"The first story, man? How should I know?"

"Well, whatchoo written about?"

"Not much. What do you find interesting about this place?"

"I dunno."

"Can you think of anything interesting in this place?"

"Plenty. You been to the other hotel, up yonder?" He pointed in one direction or another. It didn't matter.

"There's a hotel that way?"

"Man, any which way I point there's a hotel. It's downtown Atlanta."

"How about this: I'll follow you. When we stop, we stop."

"Want me to take pictures along the way?"

"Obviously."

"Word."

With that, Sylvester set out for the stairs and we began our descent into the heart of darkness.

After a floor and a half I could feel my wind leaving me.

"You realize we're nine floors up. Why couldn't we just take the elevator?"

"Elevator's crazy, dude. Takes half hour to get an elevator to go down five minutes a' stairs when there's this many people around. Besides, people don't exactly like folk like me in the elevator."

"Like you? What? Like black people? You can't blame them for that. If they had their way, they'd still have you in chains. They're just stupid, simple people."

"Naw, man. Homeless people. Sure, I get plenty of looks and judgments for bein' black, but it don't matter what color you are if you can't take a shower and you smell like something the cat drug in. It's better to just take the stairs and not deal wit' it."

"Never thought of it that way."

"Nobody does."

His odor hadn't bothered me any more than anyone else here. Maybe I was just used to it because it's probably how I smelled.

Somehow he knew which floor we were getting out of this shaft at. It must have been a sixth sense of some sort because the door we used for our exit wasn't marked and looked exactly like every other door we'd passed in the stairwell.

We came out on the mezzanine, just above the lobby party. I came to the balcony railing and looked out over the sea of multicolored heads, imagining each one was a pill with a different effect, each could cure a different symptom or drive you mad with side effects. People that come into your life contaminate it with their unique properties much like a medicine. The trick is to find people to bring in that have more beneficial reactions to your unique chemistry than side effects. In turn, you need to find someone who doesn't react to your chemistry like poison.

Alchemy.

That's what everything comes down to.

There was a soft tap on my shoulder. "C'mon, man. Let's head this way."

Sylvester turned me around and guided me to a portal that led to who knows where. White bars and girders, blue glass. It looked like something out of *2001: A Space Odyssey*. It was a portal to somewhere, but who knew where.

As we came through it, the temperature rose in the corridor; the sun came through the glass in massive shafts of light that became trapped inside as heat.

The sky-lit hallway was filled with costumed convention goers and people dressed in an assortment of loud civilian clothes. As we passed, one adorable young girl caught my eye. She was short, rail thin, and sporting a tiny skirt. She wore a plush backpack shaped like a gremlin that confused me, but I was mesmerized by the way she walked.

That was the most pleasant part of the walk through that corridor. The worst was a cadre of men, boys really, dressed in a way that was unsettling even to me. They were dressed in sports jerseys of some type. A few of them wore hats with Greek letters on them.

Frat boys.

If there was anything I understood less than all of this geek shit it was sports and frat boys. Geeks and sports loving frat boys were never a good mix.

Jocks and geeks were worse than oil and vinegar.

They were banana splits and motor oil.

It was a rivalry as old as time itself and it was punctuated firmly when the gorilla dragging his knuckles closest to the floor plowed right through my shoulder on his way by.

"Watch where you're going, you fucking mook." He probably didn't hear that last bit since I'm fairly sure I mumbled it unintelligibly. Hell, there was a pretty high chance I hadn't even said it out loud at all. Sometimes, that's just how my brain works.

Whether they heard me say anything about it or not, they still found whatever it was incredibly hilarious. They laughed hysterically at each other and my misfortune and every person passing by in costume.

They were dicks.

"Don't take it personal, Cobb. Those kinds a guys be dicks to everybody."

"I bet. Those costumes? Or are they really just meatheads?"

"They're the real deal. They rootin' for Louisiana State. There's a big game tonight. LSU verse the Tarheels."

"Hmph."

I turned and watched them leave, aghast at their behavior, until they crossed the threshold of the corridor and faded into the other hotel.

I hoped that was the last I'd see of those stupid motherfuckers.

"Fuck it. Where to, Sly?"

"This a way."

The futuristic portal we'd passed through made way to a brownstone hallway and foyer. This building was clearly built two decades before any other hotel serving as host of the convention. It was old and musty, festering with the smell of aging, cold brick to match.

The geeks pouring through the entrance were lining up for the elevators that greeted us on the other side, but Sylvester led me around to a flight of stairs. I was going to protest but I was out of breath and couldn't speak. That, and it was only one flight. Any further and I would have said, "Stink be damned, we're taking the fucking elevator."

Have I ever mentioned that I'm a lazy man and easily out of breath?

It's quite disgusting, really.

Sylvester snapped pictures of the scene the stairway door opened up to reveal. There were hundreds of con-goers crammed into the wide-open area that led to all the conference rooms this hotel had to offer.

Maybe thousands of them.

I could actually feel my blood pressure rising up from within my sternum and surging outward, causing an all-consuming tide of anxiety to ebb up over the shores of my comfort zone.

In front of me was another information kiosk. Information is exactly what I needed to ward off my fear of the unknown. So I asked the girl at the kiosk, "What the hell is all this?"

She was rail thin, flat as a board, pale in complexion, and had stringy brown hair. Just by a glance you could tell that she he had no social grace whatsoever. She had her nose buried deep into a book thicker than she was. She had to put it down to look up at me.

"Ummm?"

I waved my arm in a wide arc, indicating the hustle and bustle going on behind her. "This. All of this. What the hell is it?"

Craning her neck, she turned around to regard the scene behind her. "Oh. They're in line."

See? No social skills. That wasn't an answer, blast it, that was a preprogrammed response.

"I can see that. In line for what?"

Bryan Young

"Oh." To this poor young girl, I must have been from another planet. "Well, that one is the line for Shatner and Nimoy. That one is for Patrick Stewart. The rest are for the general autograph area line. The fire marshal said only a certain amount of people can be in that room at a time, so they let people in as others come out."

I guess if these people were giving their autographs away, it would certainly attract a crowd. "And the autographs are free?"

She chortled.

"They pay for the autographs?"

"Yeah. How else would they make money?"

I wanted so badly to be surprised by this but there wasn't much left that could shock me. In my wildest dreams I'd never understood the allure of asking someone for an autograph. What good was their signature on some piece of paper? I couldn't imagine even being asked for one, it seems like it would get annoying. But in my mind, I always assumed fans asked for autographs when they happened to meet their favorite celebrity and had the obnoxious temerity to ask for something they didn't deserve. But to pay for the privilege? And how could anyone ever be so arrogant to charge for something as simple as their signature?

It was all poppycock.

"Did you need something else, sir?"

"...fucking poppycock."

"What?"

"Huh? Oh. No. That's it."

Waving off the shapeless girl, I walked forward into the breach, Sylvester following close behind.

"Whatchoo thinkin', man?"

I was thinking that there was a story here. These people are taking advantage of their status as minor league celebrities to prey on the ignorant masses who came to this thing. I didn't care to articulate all or any of that to Sylvester, so I just kept walking toward the crowd hoping he'd follow.

There really wasn't a line that you could make out. It looked more like a holding pen for cattle. I approached a fine looking steer on the outside of the corral, a big beefy one, no less. He was three hundred pounds of guy stuffed into two hundred and fifty pounds worth of sweat pants. He was blonde and wheezed too much through gapped teeth and a thin, shabby beard. He carried an oversized portfolio

"Hey, Mongo, what's the skinny?"

"Huh?" We made eye contact so I knew he knew I was talking to him.

"What are you in line for?"

"The autograph hall."

"I can see that. Whose autograph are you trying to get?"

There was a string of names he gave me of people I didn't recognize. I'd have had an easier time if he were giving me the names of congressional pages and had asked me to match them to the offices they worked in. I probably couldn't get even an eighth of them right, but at least it would seem familiar.

Being that disconnected from what I was covering made me feel woozy.

"I don't know who they are, but~"

Mongo scoffed, "~are you living in a cave?"

Maybe I was.

He continued, "That's half the crew of Serenity, two are Imperial Officers, and then there was Captain Harriman..."

It was still over my head. All I heard was, "Something something something spaceship. Something something something movie. Something something something *Star Trek*." I was loathe to admit it, but I was at a severe disadvantage here. "You're going to have to spell it out for me, man. I've spent my career in politics. I haven't been into science fiction since middle school."

To his credit, Mongo the giant geek was very patient with me. Sure, he was stunned that a grown man could know nothing about the most exciting things in his life, but he seemed to understand instantly. Maybe he knew subconsciously that if he were to ask me about cabinet members currently serving he'd have no idea what I was talking about. He took a breath and started slowly, without a hint of patronizing, "Oh. Well, the *Serenity* was a smuggling ship on a show called *Firefly* that ran on Fox some years ago. It's very good and should have run much longer than it did. The Imperial Officers are from *Star Wars*... Well, *The Empire Strikes Back*, actually, but who doesn't love the Imperials? And Captain Harriman was the commander of the Enterprise for about 15 minutes in *Star Trek: Generations*."

I wrote all of this down. Sylvester snapped pictures of Mongo and those around him.

"Why Harriman's autograph? Why not Shatner or the other one they've got here?"

His stomach heaved and convulsed as let out a deep, genuine belly laugh.

"What's so funny?"

"Because I have money, but I don't have that kind of money."

"What kind of money?"

"Let me put it this way. For all seven autographs I want to go in there and get, I'd only be able to afford most of William Shatner's autograph. And a picture is even more."

Had I been drinking coffee, I would have spit it all over him. "Are you serious?"

Still chuckling, he nodded in the affirmative.

"Why is it so expensive?"

"He's James Tiberius Kirk. He charges what he wants and he gets it. You saw the line for it, right?"

Mongo pointed over to the far edge of the corral and a line of single file people that led up a staircase, some of them dressed in *Star Trek* uniforms. He drew my attention up to see that the line carried on down what we could see of the overhanging balcony hallway a floor above us.

"He'll probably make twenty or thirty grand in two days at this convention easy."

"Sweet fucking Jesus."

"Sweet fucking Jesus is right."

I offered my hand to shake. "Thanks for all your help, Mongo."

"My name's Dale. Dale Bradley."

"Dale? Where the fuck did I get Mongo?"

We both shrugged, thinking nothing of it.

I pulled back from the holding pen to parlay with Sylvester. "Why don't you wave your press badge around and get into that autograph hall and take some good pictures of whatever Z-level celebrities you can find."

"Where are you going?"

Rolling up my sleeves, I told him, "I'm going to have some words with William Shatner."

"Don't do anything stupid, man."

"Wouldn't dream of it."

I followed the line of uniforms up the stairs and down into the hallway. It stretched another twenty yards before turning a corner.

Before going that far, I stopped to talk to a group of people in bright red, blue and gold shirts and short-dresses. You know, just to make sure I was in the right place. "You're all here for Shatner?"

The one in the gold uniform answered for the group. He was surprisingly fit and filled the costume out nicely. Well groomed, too. If I didn't know better I would have guessed he had actually been on the show, but it had been off the air longer than he'd been alive. "Yeah, why?"

"I'm with the press, man. I've got some questions for you."

"As you please."

He stepped forward, away from the group so that we might converse easier. I pulled my notebook out as though I was going to take notes. Hell, maybe I would for a change. I was starting to feel like a new man. Worthless, to be sure, but a new and different kind of worthless. A kind of worthless I might be able to cope with.

"So, what exactly have you paid for, as you're standing here in line?"

"Well, the six of us split up the cost of a picture with Mister Shatner and Mister Nimoy."

"A picture? For all six of you?"

"We pooled our money together. Six was the max so we put together our little away team and we'll get a picture of the Captain and Science Officer with all of us."

"And the only way you guys could afford it was to get six of you together?"

"Yeah. It's pretty pricey, but he's The Captain. I can totally understand why he'd charge that. I mean... We're not anybody and he's James Tiberius Kirk."

That's the second time someone said that. Almost as though you could get away with anything if your name was James Tiberius Kirk. That's the second way to get away with murder at a convention.

"And you don't think he's exploiting his status at all? I mean, it's clear you worship him as a hero, but you don't think it's exploitative at all?"

"Exploitative?"

"He's using you."

"What?"

"Think about it. He's preying on your love and fascination for him for monetary gain."

"Isn't that what all actors do?"

"No." Well, maybe, but I wasn't conceding any ground to this hapless moron.

"I mean, we're not being used. It's capitalism. He sets a price for time and a photograph with him, and we're willing to pay that price. It's supply and demand."

Bryan Young

My eyes twitched at Herbert Lom levels when I heard the phrases "capitalism" and "supply and demand." Perhaps in the most rudimentary sense this fit some misguided notion of supply and demand, but none of the people who spout off terms like this ever seem to understand the inherent evils of "price gouging."

Thinking I'd explain it to him I took a breath, but I found that I had simply walked away in a rage. My heart was racing and I was standing in front of the security guards at the end of the line, allowing small groups of people in to see Shatner and Nimoy and get their photographs. The door was open, but any chance of seeing into the room was obscured by a black cloth hanging just inside the doorway.

The mood here was reverent. No one was speaking as they waited for their turn with their Gods. Their heads were all bowed. One at a time the security detail allowed them in after a quick briefing. They had earpieces in, presumably so they could get the word from the inside when the last group had finished. There was no exit door that I could see, which was disconcerting. Either people were exiting out a back way or were being killed in some evil Shatnerian plot.

It was time for the next briefing. The looks on the faces of those next to go in were bright and shining, as though they were going to meet their maker.

The security guard offered his speech in a low, conspiratorial tone, "As you go in, line up behind them for their photograph. Smile. You have about one minute. Be respectful. Do not ask for an autograph unless you have a ticket for an autograph and the item ready to go. Please remember that there are no questions or personal requests allowed. Above all, be quiet and respectful."

He held the curtain open for them and I caught a glimpse of Shatner and Nimoy, sitting there on stools against a brushed photography background, paying little mind to anything, even those paying their shekels to get in.

The curtain closed and the intricate ballet moved on. Over and over again, these poor little lambs went into the den of thieves to sacrifice money to their God.

It had to stop.

I tried to step my way in with the next group but the security detail must have been watching me closely. A firm hand was placed on my chest, preventing my entrance. "Whoa there, fella."

"I'm with the press. I'm here to see Shatner."

"I'm sorry, but the only way in here is if you've paid for a picture."

His voice was low and calm, maintaining his reverence and professionalism for his job. Contrary wise, my voice slowly elevated in volume. "Paid? What are you? The moneychangers? Shylock the Jew? What happened to a free press?"

"This isn't a press event, sir."

I pulled out my wallet and withdrew a hundred dollars, waving it above my head. I was practically shouting.

"Is this enough to get me in? Is it!"

"No, sir, it's not. I'm asking you kindly to please lower your voice."

"Lower my voice? This isn't a temple! I come not to bring peace but the sword for your den of thieves!"

If there were tables to overturn I would have done it. In any case, I was grabbed roughly by each arm by the well-dressed security guards and carried in the opposite direction down the hall. As they dragged me, I was shouting what must have seemed like nonsense to others but was crystal clear to me. "This is not a house of prayer, but a den of money mad pirates! Shatner is not your God!"

The security guards rounded the corner with me. I shut my mouth since I saw no reason to harangue a crowd that wasn't there.

"Sir. If you don't leave this area of the hotel immediately, I'll need you to surrender your credentials and you'll be asked to leave the convention."

"You can't do this to me."

His partner made a sour face as my breath hit his nose. "He's drunk."

"Don't you see why all of this is wrong?"

"Sir, all I see is a dumbass drunk with delusional tendencies."

I understood in short order that if I didn't wise up these guys would end my reign of terror at the convention and I still had half a dozen more stories to write. I'd lose my job and that steady paycheck.

Jesus Christ.

I was acting like a complete fucking idiot and I couldn't help it. Sure, I had every right to be outraged by all of this, but why was I being so fucking histrionic about it? Was this some lingering effect of the drugs I took? Was that even possible?

I need to tone it down a notch and choke my paranoia out. That, and I needed to quell my overriding sense of middle-class morality.

I cleared my throat and started again, hoping to convince these two gentlemen I wasn't completely bat-shit insane. "Listen. Perhaps I was a little hasty, is all. I'll be good. Just let me go. I got a little riled up and I took things a little too far. It's a little disgusting seeing those poor saps get bilked by guys who should know better and my Geiger counter for immorality and injustice was going off in my head. They're being cheated and it hurts me, is all."

"They don't see it that way."

"I can see that. But I'm at work here. Just let me go and you won't see me again."

A meaty index finger got pointed in my face, centimeters from my nose. His voice was eerily calm, "If you get within fifty yards of Mr. Shatner or Mr. Nimoy again I will personally tear you limb from limb."

"I understand. You're the archangel Gabriel, protecting the deity."

"What?"

"Nothing."

They blocked me from coming the way we came when they let me go, so I sprinted in the opposite direction until I found a stairway.

It was another forty-five minutes before I found my way back to the autograph hall. It was far too easy to get lost in this damn place. I snuck passed the security guards that protected the entrance from the massive swelling of people in line and found myself in another room full of lines.

Each of the walls were lined with tables and pictures of the celebrities sitting beneath them in their heyday. The center of the room was the same way, but with the tables pointing out. All told there must have been fifty or sixty "celebrities" signing autographs for money. All I had eyes for was the money changing hands. The sap would hand his money over to a personal-assistant-slash-cashier and they would get a ticket. They'd shuffle down to the other side of the table where the "celebrity" would accept the ticket, make a little bit of small talk with them and sign a headshot. The headshots were all from between ten and sixty years in the past, all were set against a science fiction background.

This happened over and over and over again.

Cash in, ticket out. Ticket in, worthless signature out.

Over and over and over again.

The vein in my forehead throbbed. It had to be on the cusp of exploding, spilling blood into my brain and killing me.

Or maybe it was just my overriding sense of consumer protection driven moral outrage and worsening paranoia. Or maybe it was the lingering effects of the drugs.

Who could know?

One thing was sure: I needed to find Sylvester and get the fuck out of this crazy place before I started overturning tables and releasing doves.

I needed to calm down.

I needed to get a grip.

I needed to file a story.

More than anything I needed a drink to calm my nerves and whet down the appetite of my paranoia.

Was this a withdrawal?

Damn it.

Without warning, someone from behind me clapped a firm hand down on my shoulder. I rebelled. "What the fuck do you want, man? I'll fight you if you don't get your hands off of me."

Violently, I turned around to see my would-be attacker and I put my dukes up, ready for a fight. But it was only Sylvester wearing my camera around his neck and a satisfied grin on his face.

"Shit, man. No need for rough stuff. It's just me."

"Sylvester. What the fuck are you playing at sneaking up on me like that? I could have killed you. Don't you understand? This is no place for a man in my state."

"I could tell that right off. You're sweatin' up a storm and look like you're ready to set down and die of stroke."

"Maybe I am, God damn it."

"I bet a nip a the hair a the dog that bit 'ya and a nap would do you a world a good."

Maybe he was right.

It certainly couldn't hurt.

CAPTAIN KIRK, HIGHWAY ROBBER?
By M. Cobb

Atlanta, GA - For the price of your rent for a
month, you too can come to Griffin*Con and own a
piece of science fiction history. What could
you buy at that price? A simple 8x10 photograph
with your favorite starship captain.

Other starship captains and bit players from
other film and TV franchises are in full force
across the convention hall as well, offering
pictures and autographs for sale.

Though some element of simple supply and demand
was involved, people were lined up by the thousands to pay inflated fees for autographs and
pictures with their favorite celebrities, but to
this reporter it seems like a cut and dry case
of unfair price gouging. There is certainly a
psychological element in play. Those standing
in line pervaded an acute sense of hero worship
that made this reporter feel like those preying
have an unfair advantage.

When asked if he felt the pricing was fair, one
young man in a Starfleet uniform, Dale 'Mongo'
Bradley, said, "It's pretty pricey, but he's The
Captain. I can totally understand why he'd
charge that. We're nobodies and he's somebody,
so he can do that."

As you can see, these helpless, harmless young
geeks that I've fostered a growing fondness for

are being taken advantage of by an entertainment system that abuses their sense of wonder, nostalgia, and lets anyone of sufficient status get away with highway robbery.

II

I had to hand it to Sylvester, the nip of the bottle and a nap into the evening quelled all of my anxiety and I was a new man. After the story was written and I uploaded the sixty some odd photographs Sylvester had taken, I sent him back out to take more and I nodded off.

The pictures he took weren't bad.

He got some great shots of the money changing hands in the autograph hall that if the editor were smart he'd match to my story. They were photographed almost as though they were of Senators taking bribes and I couldn't have been more proud of my choice of Sylvester for photographer. But we all knew my editor wasn't a smart man. He'd probably run the photos of the forty-year old has-been scream queen who still looked entirely fuckable. You know, the one who had barely anything to do with my story?

I'd be working for that bastard as long as I drew breath because he was giving me a steady pay check. I was forever trapped and it made me want to cry.

I tried calling Laurie again, but she didn't pick up the phone. I could only imagine that she was partying it up with her latest conquest. It was a Saturday night back home.

The saddest part is that she'd probably be doing exactly the same thing if I were there in town with her. I'd be sitting at the bar, drinking to excess as usual, while she would be off flaunting her impeccable ability to interact with members of the human race.

Interacting with humanity is still something I struggle with. Though I was beginning to come to the idea that the problem wasn't theirs, but mine.

The nap left me feeling refreshed. Filing the story made me feel accomplished. Refreshing accomplishment made me feel a might peckish.

I set out into the world, wondering how Sylvester would find me again if I wasn't where he'd left me. Quickly, I discarded that thought since I really didn't care. He was paid in cash for pictures that had already been submitted and given him a camera that the boss owned. Sure, maybe I'd feel betrayed by having him disappear after I helped him, but all he'd do at that point is solidify my distaste for the human race.

No one is reliable.

Maybe not even me.

Fuck.

The restaurant attached to the lower lobby was the closest place I could find to eat a meal. I couldn't remember the last time

I'd eaten and I didn't want to spend the next six hours looking for somewhere to eat. I was under no illusions about the fact that I would get lost if I ventured any further than the lobby without a guide. The crowd had not subsided in any meaningful way and the costumes had only grown more elaborate as the days had progressed. There was one fellow dressed as a giant yellow car-former thing that could actually box himself up into his car shape if he huddled down on the floor in the fetal position. There was another guy dressed in a full metal costume of that gay robot from *Star Wars*.

I always believe in giving credit where it's due and these guys deserved it for their enterprising use of household materials. They could turn anything in to movie replica quality costumes.

The tables at the restaurant were booked to capacity, but the overworked host offered me an open seat at the bar.

Home sweet home.

I ordered a main course of whiskey and soda with a side dish of steak and baked potatoes. Then, I worked my hardest to ignore the sports game blaring on the TV above me, hanging precariously over the bar.

It was a football game and the bright green of the field hurt my eyes almost as much as the volume of the game hurt my ears. I never understood the attraction to something so obviously retarded as football. I heard someone once say that it was a uniquely American game, because at the end of the day all it was about was the conquest of land in an exceedingly violent fashion. (Wouldn't it be European at that point? No? Probably not.) We're probably the only country left in the world with the arrogant propensity for the embrace of imperialism so long as we're the ones doing it.

Maybe my hatred of football was deeply rooted in those frequent ass kickings I'd received repeatedly in high school. For some reason I'd gotten on their bad side. I'm sure it was some horrible piece of shit that I'd done, or written in the school paper, but it didn't make the beatings any less real.

At the very least the game on the television wasn't a professional game. Professional sports irked me to no end and it was pretty obvious why. We paid these people to toss a ball around and beat the shit out of each other. It didn't make any sense. Politics was much more cutthroat and had very real consequences. And the opposition had almost always done something so diabolical that it was easy to hate them. But how could you hate an opposing sports team? They all looked exactly the same. The only difference was the color of their jerseys and their city of origin. Does it make any sense to be in a rivalry with a group of people who looked and acted and thought exactly as you did, except their team was from Cleveland and wore a puce uniform? It didn't make any sense.

All sports fans do is hate themselves.

On the other hand, maybe college sports were worse. The game on the television was a college sport. And it had all the same problems as professional sports except we were holding the promise of an education and a future over the heads of these most likely poor kids in return for beating the shit out of each other on a grass battlefield. Or a wooden battle field. Or a clay one. Or whatever the fuck else surface you could play a sport on.

It seemed to me that we were settl..
ple who thought going to battle was an easy opti..
gusting to me.

Could it be that the rowdy nature of the multitude
causing all of this festering hatred to ooze out of me?

The group around me erupted into claps and calling, one
whistled and shrieked next to my ear. There must have been a
close call by a ref or a great play or something. I was surprised
that there would be this many sports fans at a gathering for geeks.
But I looked around to see that most of the bar was full of people
in sports jerseys and purple and gold shirts and hats and other
accessories.

Where were the geeks?

Sure, there were a couple of tables of them, off in one
corner, huddled together, trying to talk to each other over the din
of the jocks, but the bar was largely filled with these meatheads.
One table full of geeks was dressed straight out of a medieval film.
Maybe Tolkien? Another was full of Stormtroopers. They were
accompanied by a couple of girls in those metal bikinis. Their
faces were nervous and terrified, the whole lot of them. They just
wanted to get their food and get the hell out of there.

I couldn't blame them.

Who could?

Ordering more whiskey grew increasingly difficult since
the cheering got increasingly out of control the longer the game
went on.

It was pretty goddamned obnoxious.

I shouted over the roar at no one in particular, "Hey, how
much longer does this fucking game have?"

167

The meatheads on either side of me gave me dirty looks
.d the bartender just pointed at the bottom of the TV. There
was a random spattering of numbers. 3rd - 01:01 - 1st and 10 and
on and on and on and on.

None of it made any sense.

"Third? There's only three periods in football, right?"

That did nothing to endear me to the guy on my right,
but the guy on my left laughed.

"You fuckin' serious, man?"

"What else would I be?"

He turned, ceasing his conversation with me.

I've found in my travels that most people don't like being
challenged and will ignore you if you do likewise. Even if they
were as big as a house. Somehow, that had worked its way into
the American character. No one stood up for themselves and
when someone finally did the most common reaction was to ignore them until they went away. It's how the government worked.

At least what I'd seen of it, anyway.

My meal finally came, along with another whiskey and
soda.

I spent the duration of my meal working hard to get into
my head and out of the bar and the sports game, which wasn't an
easy thing to do since I don't particularly like myself. I didn't
much like it any more than the raucous sports game, but at least it
was quiet in here.

I just needed to remember to keep eating and drinking
and I'd be okay.

I imagined that I was hacking at my anxiety with a battle-
axe. It was somehow in the physical form of a tree and I kept hack-

168

ing at it and hacking at it and hacking at it. I wanted my anxiety to go away, I didn't need it. Why did so many things make me uncomfortable to the point that I wanted to just stay inside and forget the world existed and get lost in my own writing?

Why was I not working on my book?

I took a moments respite, leaning on the axe-handle. I sopped up the sweat dripping from my face with a bright red handkerchief I removed from my back pocket. Tree chopping, even in the confines of my headspace, was hard, honest work. It made you appreciate where you were and where you came from. There were no gray areas in it, either. You had an axe and a tree. When the axe had met the tree enough, the tree would come down. There weren't any variables.

The heft of the axe and the thick CHUCK sound it made when it hit the tree of anxiety beckoned me and so I continued.

The tree came down and I bathed in whiskey and soda. I brought more and more whiskey and sodas into my dream world from the real world. It was raining alcoholic beverages.

Confident that I was nearing a cathartic breakthrough in my own personal psychosis, something stopped inside me. It was the roar of the crowd in the real world that interrupted and I was sucked back into it, dragged kicking and screaming.

Too bad I couldn't keep the axe.

Apparently some asshole fumbled or some shit on the last play of the game and the gold and purple team lost.

Boo-fucking-hoo.

I didn't care.

But they did. They were disappointed, pissed, and looking for people to take it out on. And the only people around were people that had spent their lives being picked on by the socially superior class of jocks.

An overly intoxicated guy in a purple cap turned sideways was screaming at the screen, pointing in an accusatory fashion, "You didn't beat us, asshole! We beat ourselves. You lost in the end! You didn't beat us, we beat ourselves!"

It was an ugly display and his friends carried him out of the lounge.

If I was reading the tea leaves right, things were going to go to hell in a hand basket so I opted to get the fuck out of there as quick as I could.

The moment my feet hit the ground and I tried moving forward I noticed that the whiskey I'd been showered with in my dreams was actually in my blood stream. Forward locomotion was fine, but I could feel that swimming in my head that told me I was just the tiniest bit outside of my body.

That's when the wall of costumes in the Marriott lobby hit me like a tidal wave. They washed over me, carrying my calm away like debris into the surf.

Anxiety cracked within, but I stopped myself. I could do one of two things: I could act like the anti-social asshole that I am and just charge through the crowd toward the elevators, hoping no one stuck a shiv in me on the way, or I could embrace it. I could just be here, comfortable in my skin. I could loosen up and try to just be okay with things.

I think these geeks had taught me a thing or two in my hours here.

Was that gratitude I felt?

Staying would force me to let go of my anger and anxiety, which was something I needed badly. Another drink and I might just be able to handle the lobby without breaking down into tears or wild hallucinations.

As long as the robotic Lincoln was nowhere to be seen, I'd be just peachy-keen and honkey-fucking-dorey.

At least that's what I hoped.

There's never any accounting for the unexpected, particularly in this place.

Drink in hand, I was ready to take over the world and for once enjoy this whole enterprise with no malice in my heart.

It felt like the rush of comfort that had come with the drugs the night before, but this time it was all me. I'd done it myself.

I'd shut off the buzz saw of anxiety and my internal self was quiet. Now I could really hear the sea of people around. Snippets were all I could hear of the conversations taking place closest to me.

To my left, a redhead dressed as a British cop in a miniskirt asked a horrifying statue, "How did you do that for the hands?"

"I just put on the nylon and painted over them with acrylic, that way I don't have to paint myself and the effect is essentially the same."

These people were speaking in tongues.

To my right a guy dressed as The Flash was talking to a black guy dressed in a red and blue leotard with a silver contraption on his head. "You don't remember me? We've met several times. I'm Antman."

"Oh, right, right. I'm not good with the Marvel characters. What are your superpowers again? You talk to ants, right?"

"Partly. Mainly I shrink down to the size of an ant while retaining my full human strength."

It was hard to imagine, mainly because I couldn't believe it myself, but I wasn't disgusted by these displays. At least they weren't hurting anybody, right?

Another one of the charitable killers in white from *Star Wars* walked directly into my point of view and placed a string of beads around my neck, as he was doing to everyone else in his general vicinity. He must have had a hundred of these plastic necklaces that he was passing out.

"You look like the droids we're looking for."

At the end of the beads was a flimsy plastic medallion. The center of the piece was a storm trooper and around it were words explaining that he was from the New Orleans garrison of the 501st. It was comforting to know it was nothing sinister. I was worried this would mark me as some sort of target in a drug-induced game of murder.

All in all it was pretty harmless. It didn't take a genius to figure out that they were just spreading a bit of their local Mardi Gras culture to the denizens of Griffin*Con. But didn't this place already have enough of that vibe?

"Show us your boobs!"

The defense rests, your honor.

The voice belonging to that last statement was behind me, so I turned in case any boobs were shown. But the scene I beheld was much different than the scene I was expecting.

One of the jocks from the restaurant was pawing at a shy young lady dressed as an elf or a Jedi or a science fiction something or other. It didn't matter. She was scantily clad and carried a light up staff. The point was she was clearly hot, clearly shy, and clearly didn't want anything to do with the jock that was shouting at her loudly to take off her bra.

"Show us your boobs," another one of them shouted at her. He was right next to her, making the volume of his request seem ludicrous. The poor girl recoiled from his words as though they were sonic bullets aimed at her face. She winced and raised her arms up to cover her body, obscuring it from the predatory gazes of the purple-clad Louisiana fans.

One of them barked at her like a dog.

No one around seemed to notice or care that this pitiable young girl was in distress. In their defense, even the most extraordinary sight in the world would seem commonplace amongst this group of misfits. To a less skeptical eye, this could just be some random piece of street theatre, a moment acted out from any number of cartoons, books, or films.

The problem with that notion was that nothing about this situation added up. We were at a geek convention and these guys were clearly sports fans and frat boys. This girl was in costume and clearly frightened. These guys looked like your standard college-age date rapists.

It all seemed so damned out of place, but no one was even looking in their direction. Everyone was carrying on as though it's completely all right.

What was I missing?

Could I be jumping to conclusions here?

I'd embarrassed myself a hundred times over during this trip and if I interceded on this young girl's behalf would it just be another blustering humiliation on my part? Would I become that screaming maniac crying wolf when none existed? Would security arrive and haul me away like the crazed fool I saw myself as?

The line in the sand was drawn for me when one of the Louisiana dick bags had snuck up behind this hapless beauty and unlatched her brassiere.

Any doubts I had about this being faked or staged were tossed out like a cup of sour coffee when she screeched and squealed like bloody murder. She reached for her falling top and scrambled to cover her exposed breasts.

They were beautiful, to be sure, but this was wrong.

Would no one else stand up for her?

Apparently not. I wasn't sure it would be me until I noticed that my fist connected with the face of the sports fan who'd disrobed her.

In his defense, it was a very weak punch and didn't do much more than make him laugh. I hadn't raised my fists for any cause since the seventh grade and was more out of practice than I would have imagined.

Fittingly, the last time I had raised my fists was to defend myself against a guy just like this. I was reliving a moment from my junior high school days, trying to defend a cheerleader from the unwanted advances from the captain of a football team.

Roughly, I was shoved and hit the ground with all the grace of a sack of kittens hitting the water. My ass was bruised as surely as my ego, but I was fine with this result because it gave the girl an opportunity to get away, which she did with all possible speed.

"Who does this guy think he is?"

They laughed.

"Who cares?"

They laughed harder.

They laughed at me, drunk out of their minds. Not just on alcohol, but hubris, too.

I was a nobody.

It was obvious I was no threat to them and their attention spans were short enough that they'd all but completely forgotten about the girl they so viciously harassed.

The job I'd done was thankless, but if the worst they were going to do with me was laugh then I could live with that, too.

Cackling like hyenas they walked away, holding their stomachs from the ache of so much laughter. They weren't just laughing at me, they were laughing at every single person in this hotel lobby in a costume, they were laughing at every person who thought it was safe to come here and act out their fantasies because they'd be amongst their own.

The thing that hurt the most, though, was that they were laughing at how pathetic I was. Here I was, trying to come to this poor girl's rescue and instead of reacting to me with the wrath of every wronged and wounded sports fanatic I was a gnat to be laughed at and shoved. I was something to be made to feel small.

It was that thought that snapped something inside of me.

Picking myself up off the ground, I dusted myself off and clenched my fist into a tight ball of anger. I was something to be reckoned with.

Following them around the fringes of the lobby and the crowd was a doubly infuriating experience. Why was I following them after such humiliation? Perhaps because I seemed to be the only one around that was cognizant of the havoc they were wreaking. Naturally, I felt obligated to make sure they didn't try to sexually assault another geeky, young girl. I could taste it in the air like the steely pallor of sea salt: they were out to debase someone and I had to, at the very least, bear witness to it if I couldn't stop it outright.

Maybe I'd be too much of a coward to intercede again though. Make no mistake: I am very much a coward. I'm a shabby, selfish person. Maybe the boiling of my moral outrage had to do with the fact that I felt protective over these geeks who had showed me something about myself. They had showed me a glimmer of who I was before all this self-loathing and for that I felt indebted to them.

The jocks stopped in front of another scantily costumed female of the incredibly attractive variety. Apparently they were so shallow that they only had eyes for ridiculous beauty that would rival that of models and movie-stars.

This girl was smooth as silk, well-tanned and well-toned. She was dressed in chain mail bikini and wore a chain around her neck.

"Hey, can we take a picture?"

"Sure," she obliged.

Four of the Louisiana frat boys huddled around her and the fifth struggled to capture the moment on his camera's phone. Just before the photo snapped, the one to her immediate right tried putting his tongue in her ear and the one to her immediate left put his hand on the bare flesh below her breast.

Her face grew long and pale with shock as she realized what was happening. She tried taking a step away, but the one on her far right had grabbed a firm hold of the chain around her neck.

"What the fuck, man?"

They all laughed at her. Just like they'd laughed at me. As though she had made the worst decision of her life to put on that costume, you could see her growing more and more self-conscious with each beat of their laughter.

Flushed, she yanked the chain firmly out of his hands and turned, walking away. Their catcalls grew in volume over the din of the crowd. The louder they got, the more defeated the slave girl became. She buried her face in her hands in tears.

But what could I do?

She walked away, crying but unscathed, and they gave each other triumphant high-fives.

"What's going down, man?"

"What the fuck is this treachery?"

A hand on my shoulder turned me around. It was Sylvester, camera around his neck.

"Settle down, it's just me, man. What's up?"

"What the fuck does it look like? Look at the swath of destruction these assholes are creating."

I stepped out of his way, assuming the path that led them away would be like the wake of a tornado. To Sylvester, I must have seemed even more unsettled and senseless than normal. The crowd had filled in behind the villains and I could see neither hide nor hair of them.

Fuck.

They were getting away.

"What?"

"They're getting away."

"Who is?"

"There's these fucking frat boys, they were in the bar watching the football game and what do they do? They lose their game and come out here and start groping pretty girls. Fucking assholes."

"That ain't surprisin'."

"We have to find them. That's the next story. We have to find them and stop them somehow."

"Stop them? How we gonna stop 'em?"

"How the fuck should I know? But they need to be stopped. You'll see. We just need to find them. And be sure to take plenty of pictures. I want to nail these fuckers to the wall."

"But how're we gonna find 'em?"

"We'll track them down like dogs, by the screams of their victims, and the cunning of our wits."

"Are you okay, man?"

"Better than I've been in a very long time."

And with that, we were on the hunt.

These fucking slime-balls had to pay for their indiscretions. A pride for these geeks swelled inside of me. Sure, we didn't always see eye to eye, but they were here and proud of what they were doing in an environment they thought was safe. It would be as if someone went to a Karaoke bar with the purpose of heckling all the singers about how bad they sucked and then touched their genitals afterwards. Sure, maybe some of them did suck but at least they were doing it in an appropriate forum. And no one deserved to feel that violated.

No one.

I've been violated. It's not pleasant... No...not like that...I mean... With Laurie. Damn it. Not like that, either. But that feeling I get when I think about how much I love her, that elation fills my heart with an optimism I've forgotten how to use. And every time she cheats on me, or won't commit to our relationship, or I catch her with another guy, it's like a giant gorilla of a jock has tapped me on the balls and put a dick so far up my ass it made my stomach hurt. It's not a pleasant experience and that's how I imagined these poor geeks felt.

I would not allow it to happen if I could help it.

It was a disgusting, dirty feeling.

I made my way past a pair of Spartan soldiers with no body armour (which doesn't even make sense when you think about it, I mean, really, talk about ridiculously, historically inaccurate... Sure they had lovely sets of abs, but really?) and proceeded on my search for the vile, jocular brigands.

And that's when he appeared.

From the crowd, there stood a man a full head taller than anyone else and his stovepipe hat extended above even that.

It was Lincoln, staring right at me with his penetrating brown eyes.

His brow furrowed when he processed my visage in his ancient, clearly immortal, brain.

"He found me. I don't know how, but he found me."

"Whatchoo talkin' about, man? Who? Who found you?"

"Abraham Lincoln..."

I pointed out to Sylvester the liberator of his ancestors and turned to run, hoping we'd be able to make a hasty escape. Clamoring past costumed convention goers, I had to get away. If he got his hands on me this time, it was sure to be all over and I couldn't let that happen, not with so much on the line.

Cold sweat was congealing on my brow. The terror of running from Honest Abe through this oversized merry-go-round was enough to still my beating heart.

I crashed through a pair of geeks dressed in cardboard boxes like a wrecking ball through a vacant building. I felt as though escape from Lincoln could have been within my reach...

...if I hadn't somehow run headlong back into the oppressing arms of the Louisiana State fans.

Running from my problems with Lincoln, I'd been delivered the providence of running (literally) into those I was seeking out to smite.

The one I'd smashed into was furious.

"Excuse me," I tried bluffing. I didn't have much of a plan, so I'd just need to distract them until I could figure out a way to get them ejected from the convention.

Where was the Incredible Hulk when you needed him? He'd smash these guys to bits.

"Don't you take a fucking hint, man?"

"Hulk smash?"

He shoved me. Hard. I staggered back, right into a pudgy girl dressed up as Alice in Wonderland. She snorted like a pig and shoved me away from her as though she were a flipper in a pinball game, trying desperately to get me away before my balls fell into her gutter. Or something.

The one I bashed into turned to his friends, calling for back up he probably didn't need. He certainly didn't need help to dispatch me, anyway. One quick right hook and I was done for.

Hell, a stiff breeze and a limp shove would do me in.

I took a pair of cowardly steps backwards, but that's when the cold sweat hit me and I tripped. Spinning around, terror struck me. Was it my head spinning, or just the room? And was that Lincoln behind me? I was trapped between two of the worst options: the Jocks I wanted to badly to teach a lesson and the ex-President who wanted to see me dead.

"It's a fucking merry-go-round."

Did I say that? Or just think it?

As I pondered the absurdity of my terrible reality, I was shoved down to the ground by a stiff, meaty hand.

A din of laughing grew around me. I was in an amusement park funhouse and all the people around me were distorted mirror reflections. They were clowns in nightmares, blood trickling from their jagged teeth.

The leader of the pack posed for a photograph with an incredibly attractive, tight-bodied young lady who may as well have been a model in her real life. She was wearing a black variation of some manner secret agent's outfit, but it was skintight and vinyl, leaving nothing of her shape to the imagination. She had a perfect hourglass figure and the details of her costume made it all the more sensual and revealing. Her neckline plunged to a deep point beyond her mesmerizing cleavage, which drew the eye to her bright yellow belt where a prop gun rested gently in a holster.

Bryan Young

She had a flowing mane of bright red hair and her makeup seemed as though a master had applied it.

The only thing more attractive than her body and attire was her body language. Each tiny move and imperceptible gesture dripped with sex.

Whether that was her natural state or she was playing a character, it didn't matter. She was absolutely beautiful and these ne'r-do-wells were going to do something she'd never forget for the rest of her life.

In the space of a blink, that moment between the photographer idiotically requesting they say cheese and the flash of the camera, the scene turned from standard convention fare to sexual assault.

The leader of the wolves in purple roughly snatched her dignity, grabbing her left breast tightly with one hand and squeezing her vagina with the other.

To add insult to grave injury, he stuck his tongue out, capturing forever on film (or digital or whatever) his brutal attack on this young lady.

The shock of it all took what felt like an eternity to sink in, not just to the girl, but to the wolves. The difference was that she knew there had been a line crossed and to them, it was all just another joke.

Fucking sociopaths.

As soon as it dawned on her, she slapped her aggressor across the face with an open palm and leapt back, getting as much distance between her and them as possible.

But it wasn't enough.

Though his crew responded with their signature laughter, their fearless leader was angry and lashed out, shoving the poor girl backwards into the crowd.

Flailing back, she smashed right into one of the overly athletic entourage and I knew I could not let this aggression stand.

Heaving air into my chest, I rose to my feet, feeling invincible. A hand helped me up, Sylvester's most likely, but I shook it off. I could do this on my own. My shoulders straightened, my head raised high, and with heavy marching steps I walked right up to the King of the Dickheads and firmly planted my fist into the right side of his face with all the force I could muster.

I may as well have been punching a wall of solid steel with a feather pillow.

A wall of steel would have been preferable, though, because walls of steel don't hit back.

When his knuckles met with the front of my jaw, I knew I would be feeling it for a long time and no amount of ice and alcohol was going to dull the pain. The force of the blow spun me around and dazzled bright flashing stars in my field of view.

To my eternal gratitude, Sylvester had my back. Instead of reeling into another enemy like a bumper in that pinball machine, Sylvester snagged that would be bumper, turned him on his heels and cracked him with an impressive haymaker.

My collar was grabbed and I was yanked in close to one of the infidels. We were nose to nose.

"You sons of bitches!"

I'm guessing that was me, begging to be hit.

"What the fuck is wrong with you? You can't do this shit."

Fuck. That was definitely me. Was I just trying to get my foot in my mouth before they had a chance to fill it with their fists?

"What the fuck is your problem, old man?" He slurred his words through too much alcohol, so it came out more like, "...'t the fuck'sh yer problem, old man?"

"You're my problem. You're out of control and you need to be stopped." My words came out as though I'd been reading as many comic books as those I was so eager to protect. I sounded like a costumed vigilante. Now if only I had a mask and a sword...

My captor let me go and wound his fist, but I was determined to stand fast and take it. Closing my eyes, I cringed, waiting for it to crush me, smashing my face from a new direction.

But the blow never came.

The only thing that came was a smooth, deep voice in an Illinois drawl, "A house divided against itself cannot stand."

"What?"

I cracked my eyes open just enough to see that a fist was *not* about to clobber my face into oblivion, but that the strong, steam powered hand of Abraham Lincoln was holding the threatening fist back and had pulled his other cybernetically enhanced hand back into a fist of its own.

With all the fury and blinding grace of God, the sixteenth President of the United States of America used his mighty fist to explode the nose of my oppressor into a mess of shattered bones and bloody pulp.

It was to my good fortune that I avoided Lincoln's wrath for so long. Clearly, he was a more than formidable opponent than I thought and trained in the ways of gentlemanly combat.

Before I could even think to ask what he was doing defending me, he said loudly into my general direction, "A friend is one who has the same enemies as you have."

Something jerked me back, out of the way of one of the confederates that had seen fit to charge me like a bull. He missed me as if I had been a lucky matador, but he bowled into his comrades. They were furious and regrouping, red daggers in their eyes, aimed squarely across the opening in the crowd at their opponents.

In their matching violet sports getup and Greek lettered hats they looked like a well oiled fighting team, ready to take all comers. The three of us stood together. A drunk journalist, a homeless photographer, and a mechanically re-engineered former president. It was the most disharmonious and unlikely ragtag defenders of justice that Griffin*Con—nay, the entire world—had ever seen.

The purple-jacketed warriors had dusted themselves off, wiped the blood from their noses, and were rolling up their sleeves.

It was quite clear they would destroy us if there was going to be a standup fight.

Something gave me pause, though. Why did no one crowd we were in the midst of seem to care of the duel occurring right around them? Looking around, it was clear that even the young girl they'd assaulted had disappeared.

Maybe she was the smart one.

It was Sylvester who broke the silence, "We need to get outta here."

I wasn't going to argue. The last thing I could afford was a hospital bill.

It was Lincoln's call, though. He was certainly the biggest bruiser of the group. "We'll go, gentlemen. But we're not retreating. We're advancing in a different direction."

On his lead, we turned and ran.

In hot pursuit behind us, the leader of the ratfinks shouted, "We're gonna beat your fucking asses!"

I believed him.

Making it through the crowd was difficult, very much like I imagined swimming upstream in molasses would be. I don't know why that was the image that came to mind. I was hoping for something more violent, something that would buck me up against the coming fight if they caught us.

It was my good luck that Lincoln seemed able to see right over the crowd and could guide us through it. The jocks behind us were having much the same problems though. Getting through this mess was damn near impossible at any meaningful speed.

To Lincoln's credit, he seemed to have an eye for every opening that would give our retreat an advantage and we were moving as unobtrusively through the costumed crowd as we could, though we ran through so many groups posing for pictures that the sides of our heads must have made it into dozens of photographs.

The jocks, on the other hand, were simply shoving people out of their way in order to get to us. Our way was sleek, theirs was much more brutal.

There were a few times I looked behind to see them coming up fast, but Lincoln seemed to know where he was going. I prayed he knew where he was going. We could have been going in circles for all I knew, all I could see around me were assholes in bright spandex and plastic armour. As far as I could tell, my surroundings hadn't changed, but Lincoln seemed confident so I trusted him. I had to trust him or I'd fall by the wayside and be torn to shreds by the rabid wolves behind me.

"Get the fuck back here!"

"Get fucked, asshat!" That was me, telling them where they could stick it.

It probably wasn't wise to egg them on, but it was in my nature.

"I'm gonna fuckin' pound the shit out of you, assholes!"

Now they were really getting angry. I have that effect on people.

"Fags!"

That was all I had breath enough to shout behind me and it would rile them up even further. I can't imagine anything that could piss a virile, young, hyper-heterosexual, frat boy off more than insinuating that they're homosexuals.

It's probably because they secretly really did want cocks in their mouths and in their assholes.

Which is totally cool with me. It's not how I roll, but if they wanted cock, far be it from me to argue.

"Cocksuckers!"

We broke through the edge of the crowd and it was like we'd reached the edge of Earth's gravity, cruising through space at breakaway speed.

Lincoln led us at a full sprint down a hallway I didn't recognize, though I fully admit I'd probably been through it before a dozen times.

It was through a pair of guys dressed as Batman, each from a different era, that the jocks crashed through the crowd. It's a humbling experience to see Batman knocked to the ground and run over by a gang of angered morons.

Now that we were making forward momentum at a sprinting pace, I carried on, assuming Lincoln had a destination in mind. Though for all I knew, he could have just been trying to wear them out.

My lungs ached and burned from the effort. I wanted to collapse and wheeze until my breathing normalized, but that would clearly result in me being put into traction.

These assholes wanted to kill me. They wanted to kill all of us, we three defenders of the geeks.

Maybe they would. In public even. If I weren't trying so hard to keep out of the hands of those who would murder me happily, I'd have shrugged.

To keep my mind off the thick smoldering sensation in my lungs, I imagined myself as the hunter instead of the hunted.

The weight of a thick spear in my hands and a quiver of them on my back felt good. It was a horrible thing to imagine, the sharp end of the stick being thrown at a full velocity and piercing into the back of the jock closest too me. He fell, dropping into the crowd and spilling his own blood onto the carpet in a bubbling mess like thick, red maple syrup.

My next spear flew straight and true, right through one of their heads. It skewered through his brain like a sword through a watermelon.

It wasn't until I tripped in reality that I snapped myself out of my wonderful dream. My foot had snagged a bundle of cables that had appeared beneath me. My chin had hit the ground, letting out a shrill ringing in my ears and an intense pain reverberating through my head.

It was a hell of a wake up call and things had changed drastically since I'd checked out.

To my left was a seated crowd and to my right was a brightly lit stage. At the foot of the stage, off to one side, was a podium and some person or another was holding court over the audience. Behind him, over the field of the theater, was a group of people in costumes in the middle of a dance number.

Sylvester and Lincoln seemed to realize that I'd gone down and turned, coming back for me. It was fortunate that I'd actually followed them in my daze. I could have split off and gone anywhere.

As they came back for me, cringing looks of horror pulled their faces back and reminded me why we were running in the first place.

Rolling over to my back, I lifted my head to see our pursuers, coming straight at me, pressing the advantage of my fall to the fullest extent.

In short, we were fucked.

My companions raced right by me and met our foes in single combat as though they were gladiators in an arena. That analogy was much more apt when I realized we were being watched from all sides and I was reasonably certain there were cameras trained on us as well.

Lincoln gave out a shrill war-whoop that I recognized at once to be the Rebel Yell. I could not think of anything more unnerving than Lincoln entering into battle against these cock-suckers with a confidence shaking Confederate war cry.

Sadly, the cognitive dissonance of the thing was unsettling only to me. These jocks were drunk fucking idiots.

"Woo! Whooo-woo-hoo!"

One of them clocked Lincoln in the face and another kicked Sylvester.

A flash in my brain imagined the fist hitting Honest Abe as the same one grabbing that poor girl's lady bits and my blood was boiling.

Scrambling to my feet I was going to make damn sure this was going to be an all out brawl to be long remembered. They'd sing of this day.

I set my sights on the leader, vowing to do as much damage to him as I could muster. I wasn't a strong man, but I had scraggly nails and sharp teeth and could do plenty of wounding damage if I could get close enough without getting knocked the fuck out.

I probably wasn't going to be much help, but I couldn't let Sylvester and Lincoln fight this battle without me.

How could I?

They stepped up to help me even though I'm a god-damned son of a bitch.

Maybe I was asking myself the same question in my head to keep from joining the fray, but, like a skipping record, all I needed was a nudge and I was back on track. That nudge came in the form of the solid impact of a fist with Sylvester's face, spraying homeless blood in my direction.

"That's it, mother fuckers."

Before I knew it was happening my fists were flying furiously. I was in one of the badly dubbed Kung Fu movies I had loved so dearly in my youth. I was a slice of half a loaf of Kung Fu.

My arm straightened and the points of my knuckles met the sharp blade of a noise in the middle of their leader's face.

For once, I could feel the weight of my blow actually affect the target, making me wonder if I was day-dreaming or not. Honestly, I couldn't tell. In reality, any attempt for me to commit violence of any sort was accompanied by a wobbly feeling in my knees and any punches I'd try to throw had no force behind them. My reality was that dream you'd always have where you could never scream and blows were harmless.

But this time my target's head recoiled with the force of my blow and I could have sworn I wasn't in the real world.

That assumption was proven wrong pretty fucking quickly. In my violent daydreams I'd never been hurt in any way, but now a rough hand had grabbed my wrist, turned my body around, and I could feel the dull pain of a quick thump to my kidneys.

Jesus Christ.

No wonder I hated fighting. It fucking hurt. Bad.

The pig-like squealing that filled the air may or may not have been me.

A meaty forearm made its way around my neck, trying to shut me up, but I knew exactly what to do in this situation. I took in a mouthful of dumbass and clamped down with my teeth.

"Mother fucker," someone shouted.

I got spun around again like a top and took a painful uppercut to my already sore jaw, knocking my ass to the ground.

On my way to the ground, and with some extra ability beyond me, I took note of the situation Lincoln and Sylvester had found themselves in.

Sylvester was being held up by two of the meatheads and taking a vicious thrashing at the hands of a third. My heart felt for him, but I was useless and I was starting to remember why.

Space Lincoln, on the other hand, was faring much better than my homeless companion. I'm confident his mechanical arms gave him an edge that allowed him to hold out much longer than Sly and I. He was delivering blow after blow to different opponents, bobbing and weaving, shucking and jiving, like Muhammad fucking Ali.

Left jab, left jab, right hook, left hook, uppercut, mother fuckin' knock out.

He made me feel almost like we'd get out of this on top.

Almost.

I hit the ground hard and the dick face that knocked me down jumped up onto Lincolns back as though he were offering him a piggyback ride.

The last of the group came over as though he were going to exploit the situation, but I thrust my leg into his way, tripping him good. His face collided with the carpet with all the concussive force of the Little Boy that rocked Hiroshima.

Things got blurry from that point.

Sylvester leveraged one of his tormentors down on top of the one I'd tripped, but then he was yanked down himself. I rolled around and started looking for more flesh to bite or scratch, adding myself to the pile. Sometime between then and my next fleshy bite, Lincoln had come down on top of us, as well as the rest of the jocks.

To the audience in attendance, or those watching us from the comfort of their hotel room, we must have looked like one of those scraggly dust clouds of violence you'd see during an old cartoon.

We were writhing in collective anger, trying to do as much damage to each other as we could before something ended it once and for all.

I took a hit from one side, got tapped in the balls with a foot from another side, I dug my nails into some exposed, doughy flesh over here, I kicked a face over there.

The collective amount of adrenaline in the dog pile must have been off the chart, we all fought like men possessed. None more so than Sylvester, Space Lincoln, and myself, though. We had actual, legitimate moral superiority on our side. We were right. We were fighting for Right. For Justice.

We three, Defenders of the Geeks. We were mother-fucking superheroes fighting the evil, spoiled, silver-spoon toting frat boys of the world's seedy underbelly. We were striking a blow for all that was good and holy in the world.

The only problem was that we were getting our asses beat and there really wasn't much we could do about it. We were out-numbered two-to-one, they were physically superior models, what with all of their meat-headed sports training, and they were more experienced fighters.

And I don't mean we were losing by a margin. We were losing by a damn sight. Blow after blow registered on my fragile body until I was just a bundle of bruised hurt and I couldn't imagine Abe and Sly feeling any better than I did.

It was a lot more hurt than some alcohol and ibuprofen were going to be fixed by in the morning, I could tell you that.

But we stood fast, never backing down.

I almost got to my feet twice, hoping that if I stood I could rally some of the crowd to our cause. We wouldn't be so outnumbered if the countless thousands in the hall came to our aid. Sadly, I had my legs roughly hewn from beneath me each time I tried doing as such. It made me sad that the audience didn't join in on this cathartic beat down themselves.

What sort of damaged mind watches this sort of carnage unfold and doesn't understand enough to intercede on behalf of their losing protectors? It was unconscionable. More than that, it was infuriating. Why was I fighting for these assholes if they wouldn't fight for themselves?

I abhor violence as much as the next guy, more so even, and here I was, standing up for something.

That's when I remembered why we got into this whole mess in the first place. The beautiful female spy who'd been touched inappropriately by the leader of the jocks appeared. She entered the room with a phalanx of armed security with her.

Looking as incredibly attractive as ever, she fingered the perpetrators to the cops and they quickly responded by wrestling them out of the pile and handcuffing them one by one. It wasn't an easy process and I was glad to see the cops get a couple of good punches in.

It was assumed that she explained to the cops what my companions and I were up to since they didn't throw us in handcuffs, too. For the fact that we weren't specifically hassled and arrested I was grateful.

Battered and limping, it was Space Lincoln who was the first to rise to his feet and, under his own locomotion. He hobbled toward the stage with singular purpose.

"Help me up here, son," he whispered to the Master of Ceremonies of whatever event that we had just crashed. They quickly obliged, helping him up to the raised dais of the stage.

All eyes in the room were on him.

Slowly, he smoothed his walking pattern and approached the microphone and podium.

He cleared his throat.

This was going to be good.

A snare of feedback shot through the speakers as he began to speak, but he stopped, tapped the mic, and cleared his throat. His thick mechanical hands found purchase on the straps keeping the mechanics of his backpack firmly on his person. He spoke in that low country drawl that we all assumed Lincoln ought to sound like, but his words came in fits and starts. He was clearly tired and he obviously hadn't prepared his speech.

"Two all too brief days ago convention organizers brought forth in this hotel a place where those of us so inclined could congregate without fear of reproach or reprisal. In this wondrous place, we gather each year to show off the fruits of our craftsmanship and to assemble with like-minded patrons of the science fiction arts."

The audience was drinking it in. He took a moment, turning his head to pop his neck, and began once more. "This evening, individuals who understood not our ways invaded our humble sanctuary, took advantage of the generous nature of our spirits and brought judgment, harsh intemperance, and touched the spirit and flesh of our own inappropriately and viciously."

He coughed and cleared his throat. His eyes scanned the audience, connecting with each and every soul in the room. Mine most of all.

"In the halls of this auditorium we come each year to honor the achievements of our masquerading brethren, but there are a few, a proud and chosen few, who stood up today to defend us and our way of life."

Oh, shit.

He was talking about me and Sylvester.

Lincoln extended his arm and offered us to the crowd. They were confused. They were probably even more confused than I was. Can you imagine what this all must have looked like from their perspective? One minute they're watching a group of their fellows cavorting in costume on stage in their equivalent of the costume Oscars and all of a sudden Abraham Lincoln, a homeless man, and an asshole, dash into the room at top speed, chased by a gaggle of douchebags in matching purple and gold. Suddenly the asshole face plants and all hell breaks loose.

The whirling dervish of a fight dissipates, the mechanical remains of Abraham Lincoln stands, dusts himself off and offers a speech of bizarre eloquence and points to us as heroes.

It took a moment for them to comprehend Lincoln's words. I'd be stunned too, if I were them. Was he serious? Were we just a part of the show?

It didn't matter; they'd all just witnessed something they would never forget for the rest of their lives.

And they stood, erupting into clapter. Which I know isn't a word, but it should be, so I used it anyway.

It's difficult to describe what it felt to have somehow earned the approval of so many people all at once. A warmth rose in me, starting deep in the pit of my chest and rising up through my beating heart and culminating in an overwhelming sense of personal satisfaction. Perhaps it had leaked from my eyes just a bit.

I suppose it was a feeling I could get used to.

Once the bewildered applause subsided, Lincoln had collected his thoughts and went back to his speechifying. "We have had our problems with those who would oppress us for the whole of our lives, but I hope the courage shown by these men will be a shimmering example for us. That we would put aside the fear we feel for those who assert an unjust superiority over us and stand up to them, and that our support of each other and those like us shall not perish from this earth. Not now. Not ever."

He even had Lincoln's knack for turning a phrase and giving you the chills. This guy was good. I had to give him that.

The crowd started their applause once more, but I had the feeling we'd be overstaying our welcome. Maybe they weren't so interested in cheering me as the sentiment. This was a sacred place to many of them and these cheese dick jocks did their best to turn it back into their high school experience all over again.

That was the only explanation, right? They were playing out their dominance over these nerds, but the difference was the nerds had blossomed into beautiful people and were not only fit for dominating, but for violating. Perhaps in their minds, they just watched their high school bullies receive their comeuppance.

The cops, brought by the violated young lady, were eyeing me as though the wanted to talk to me, which was my cue to leave. They had gathered at the far side of the room to figure out what happened, right behind a seven-foot monstrosity dressed in a drab gray robe and a thick and menacing pewter mask. He carried a mace with a thick armoured hand with a pronounced gold ring around his middle finger.

He must have been their enforcer.

Mangled as badly as I was, Sylvester and I leaned on each other on our way to the door. Lincoln joined us when he came off the stage.

The master of ceremonies reclaimed the podium and stammered like an idiot. "Uhh...um..."

Something about the entire situation was hilarious, something about the un-believability of it all.

"Uh, without further ado, I suppose we'll move onto our next entrant in the Masquerade..."

Though we chose the back door, the cops and security guards followed us out. Sure, my body was already fucked, completely racked with creaking pain, but these guys were going to do the real damage, weren't they?

"Hold on there."

"Who? Me?" I hoped that if I played dumb they'd forget about the whole thing.

No such luck.

"Yeah. You want to come talk to us for a minute?"

"No."

But that answer wasn't good enough.

Sylvester whispered into my ear, "Shit, man, trouble with the law won't be good for me, man."

"Me neither," I whispered back, "but it doesn't look like we have much of a choice."

"Fuck."

Fuck was right.

When we opened the back door that let out into a suspiciously familiar lobby area, we could see a whole cadre of law enforcement and I knew there was no getting out of this.

If I went to jail, I went to jail. It would be worth it to have given those fucktards what for. I was perfectly capable of suffering the consequences of my actions. I still didn't want to, but I was capable of doing so.

The brawny cop, the one who was so barrel-chested he barely fit into his uniform, waved us over. I thought about running, but I couldn't breathe. I was hot and sweaty. I could feel scratches, bites, and bruises all over my body, stinging me with every step. Running was out of the question.

These cops would probably shoot me in the back if I tried to run anyway. What else would they do? I was in the company of a homeless black man and a man notorious for having been shot in the back. I stood no chance if we decided to cheese it, so I simply acquiesced.

"So, you wanna tell us what happened over there?"

Lincoln seemed to be our de facto leader, so the questions were addressed to him.

The steam powered former president explained the situation to the officers and they were incredibly agreeable. Perhaps it had something to do with the fact that the word of Abraham Lincoln, mechanically enhanced or not, was somehow above reproach and begged to be believed, no matter how absurd.

Few situations could have been more absurd than this.

The brawny officer wrote down every detail he could in his notebook as Abe told it. He was a stunning orator and just hearing about what had happened all over again boiled over the pot of the adrenaline in my system. Listening to him tell it, I couldn't believe I'd been part of something that sounded so normal and noble.

It must not have been me.

I couldn't have done something so selfless. I was the most selfish mother-fucker I knew. Well, maybe not as selfish as Laurie seemed to be. Maybe her problem with me wasn't her fault, like I've been thinking. Maybe it was mine.

The way Lincoln spun the story to the police made it seem as though he was leading them away from the crowds. They were angry enough and trying to start a fight and Lincoln felt the best thing to do was draw them away from the multitudes. He made it sound as though we were simply dangling keys in front of high-powered infants so no one else would get hurt.

The cop turned to me and asked in a thick Georgian drawl, "What made you decide to get involved?"

I was instantly disarmed.

I was thinking about what I was doing, rationalizing it, but for the life of me I can't figure out why I risked my neck for anyone else. Sure, I was an asshole when it came to down to me personally, but I was a liberal Robin Hood when it came to public policy when I wrote opinion pieces. I have genuinely felt for the whole of my life that helping others was an imperative, but I always wanted to stay out of it. As a journalist, how could I step in? All I had to do was remain passive, apathetic, and let others do the acting.

Were my actions a result of being too drunk to put my walls up?

No. I've been far more drunk and backed away from getting involved in much more heinous acts, particularly during that stint as a war correspondent. No, something inside me was different and I couldn't figure out what it was.

I didn't have a proper answer for the cop.

"I couldn't help myself."

That was as honest and accurate an answer as I could summon.

For the most part, the sweat from our struggle had subsided, so it was odd to me that Sylvester was still perspiring nervously. Through a wheeze, he coughed and looked away, avoiding eye contact with the police.

Without looking up from his notepad, the officer asked, "Can I get some identification from you three?"

I swear Sylvester looked like a deer in headlights, though that's a cliché and I try to stay away from them. Or I don't. Whatever. In either case, he looked as though the fear of God was put into him and he didn't know if he should shit or go blind.

How's that for clichés?

I wondered what it was that could have caused so much consternation for him, but then I wondered if his story about being down on his luck was going to have a much more sinister turn than I had imagined. What would a check of his ID reveal? Did he abscond with the church funds? Was he an escaped convict? I'd like to think that he'd killed a man, that's the romantic in me.

It didn't matter to me what he'd done before, if he'd done anything at all. He did me a favor, had showed me real kindness and loyalty. I couldn't just let these pigs put the fucking leeches on him.

From its home in my back pocket, I pulled the out-of-state drivers license from my wallet and handed it to the officer. Lincoln produced an impressive, leather billfold from the inner pocket of his coat and handed over an Illinois license to the cop.

"What about you?" The cop was pointing right at Sylvester.

Before Sylvester could answer, I made a casual step between him and the cop. "He works for me. He left his license up in the room. I can vouch for him. He's my photographer."

Sylvester raised the camera up to reinforce the point. Only then did I notice that the lens had been cracked and the housing smashed. It was a digital number and God only knew if I'd be able to get the photographs I needed off the damn thing. But it didn't matter, what I had was a great story.

No. That's not quite right. Maybe I didn't have a great story, but it didn't matter because I had finally found perspective, which is almost as good as a great story.

With enough perspective and the right point of view, perhaps any story could be great.

My photographer tensed, holding his breath in, waiting to see if my ruse would work.

The officer wrote my license number down on his pad. Which was fine with me, I didn't have anything on my record. For all of my shitty ways, I stayed pretty clean. I stayed clean mainly because I'd be too annoyed to deal with the consequences of doing anything extremely idiotic. Can you imagine having to go through the hassle of going to court for something as retarded as a bar fight or criminal mischief?

He slipped my license underneath Lincoln's and took in the information. Surprised, he did a double take between the license and Abe's face. He was skeptical of the man in front of him, thought better of caring, then smirked and continued writing the license number down.

When he finished, he handed me my license back, "Mr. Cobb."

Comparing the mechanical marvel of a man before him one last time to his ID, he finally handed Lincoln his license back, too. "Mr. President."

The officer locked eyes with Sylvester, and Sylvester shrank like a wilting flower beneath his glare. "Something wrong?"

"He just took a beating at the hands of those cocksuckers, of course something's wrong."

"Right." Somehow, that answer worked for the cop. "There's a paramedic on the way if you guys want to see them. Wait right here for a minute."

The officer strolled back to the group of his fellow cops and they powwowed about whatever it is cops discuss in the midst of whatever it is they thought of this whole goddamned situation.

Sylvester let his breath out and mopped the sweat off his face with his sleeve. "Thanks, man," he whispered to me.

"Why were you so worried about it?"

"I ain't got no ID. I'm nobody. And they don't like no-bodies.'

"So you don't have any warrants?"

"Not unless the credit card companies and the banks are out for blood."

"So you didn't kill anyone?"

"Huh?"

"Nevermind."

"I'm not so sure I wanna stay around for the paramedics, man."

"Why not?"

"I don't want no more bounties on my head cuz I can't pay 'em."

The annoyed outrage in my chest growled out my throat. There were few things more disgusting than someone turning down medical care because they were worried about bill collectors. But that's a whole different story, one that would only just piss me the fuck off.

But that's what gave me an idea.

"Why don't you stay? You should get the paramedics to document everything they did to you so you can sue the shit out of those fuckers. Damages and everything. You might be able to make a tidy little profit out of this, maybe get back on your feet."

He mulled it over for a minute, thinking about it. "That ain't a bad idea, but that ain't my style, you know?"

"Isn't that the American way?"

"Maybe it is. And maybe I should. But it don't feel honest."

That's when Lincoln put a mechanized arm on Sylvester's shoulder and asked him his name. "Well, Sylvester, you need to do what you feel is right, of course. Though I must say, the American way is based on justice and equality. And those boys certainly deserve to be meted justice. My firm feeling is that the law would be on your side if you chose to take that long and difficult road toward litigation."

"Well, maybe..."

"In any case, it's time for me to go. There's things to do and I've tarried a while too long in all of this business. Though I'm bruised and battered, our work was good and well rewarding. And the pair of you have impressed me more than the whole of all the others here, for you stood up for justice despite facing insurmountable odds against a foe beyond you. It was a selfless act, and I hope good fortune finds you for your deeds."

He shook each Sylvester's hand and said, "It was my honor to fight by your side, sir."

He turned to me then and embraced my hand firmly. "And you, Jeff, welcome to the club."

"What club is that?"

"I think you know."

He let go of my hand, regarded us both with that half smile of his and left. Something nagged at me, wondering if I'd ever see him again.

Sylvester noted as Lincoln disappeared into the milieu, "Dude's costume is outta sight."

I'm not sure what he meant by that, but he was homeless. What did he know?

"I may just wait for the paramedics, man."

"Splendid."

"I guess this is it." Sylvester raised his hand to shake mine, but I refused it.

"Nah. I still have the room for tonight. The floor's still yours if you want it."

"I'd appreciate that, man. Like you wouldn't believe."

"Somehow, I think I would."

The paramedics had arrived at that point and it took some convincing that they didn't need to treat me. I looked as bad as I felt and they wanted to at least treat my cuts and bruises and check me out.

I didn't let them.

Fucking bastards.

I left while they gave Sylvester the whole nine yards, though, which was good for him. Poor bastard probably hadn't seen a doctor in years. Who knows what they'd find beside the battle scars? Anything really.

I once ran into a homeless guy that had the most grotesque disfiguration. He appeared by bicycle from out of nowhere on the top level of a parking garage. It was very weird. But he came up to me and launched into his schtick for panhandling: he lifted up his shirt to reveal this horrible hernia type growth on his stomach. It might have been the most disgusting thing I'd ever seen. With each breath the growth would bubble up and down like a balloon. He might have been growing a clone out of his navel for all I knew. I gave the daffy fucker five bucks just to put his shirt down and get the fuck away from me. But his whole pitch was predicated on the fact that he couldn't afford to see a doctor.

Still pisses me off when I think about it. Not that I was duped into giving the poor bastard five bucks, but that he couldn't afford to have it looked at. Maybe he could have got help in a shelter, I don't fucking know.

What I do know is that it was depressing.

I walked back to my room, trying my hardest not to think about the time it took me to get there.

My eyes were closed and I was off in slumberland long before my head finally hit the pillow.

GEEKS VS. JOCKS: A BRAWL BREAKS OUT AT
GRIFFIN*CON
By M. Cobb

ATLANTA, GA - If one thinks back to their days
in high school, it's almost certain that one
will remember the cliques that existed. No two
cliques were more at odds than the geeks and the
jocks.

Never has that divide been more apparent than
during the evening's festivities at Griffin*Con
this evening. Though neither team resides in Atlanta, the game between the Louisiana State Ti-
gers and the North Carolina Tarheels attracted a
crowd to the convention's restaurants and bars.

A cadre of Louisiana fans found themselves deep
in the heart of Griffin*Con's costumed denizens
after the results of their game were in and
their beloved team had lost. Angry and drunk,
they stormed the costumed denizens of
Griffin*Con at the height of their annual party,
creating a mixture much like oil and vinegar.

The drunken Louisiana fans were incarcerated after sexually assaulting a scantily dressed female convention-goer, and then brutally attack-
ing three men who came to her aid. One appeared
to be the sixteenth President of the United
States, Abraham Lincoln, with mechanical enhancements to his arms and over his would-be
bullet wounds.

The brawl ended in front of the audience of the Masquerade, the annual Griffin*Con costume contest. Cameras were filming, and *Titan* is working to get the footage for review. There has been no word whether or not the fight went out live.

This merely serves to highlight the age-old battle. When asked about it, Mary Todd, a frequent visitor of Griffin*Con said, "It's really sad. I had to hide who I was so I could be popular in high school and when people did find out, it caused me all kinds of trouble. I was shunned, ostracized, made fun of. But as an adult, I'm able to come to Griffin*Con and be who I am without worrying about people judging me. These guys changed that."

A man who witnessed the sexual assault commented, "It was really crass what these guys did. They were trying to take pictures with the girls, but just before they'd snap the photo, they'd lick them and touch their lady parts and grab their boobs. It was way out of line."

The concerned con-goers who interceded on behalf of the young girls refused to identify themselves and offered only a brief comment on the situation, "These guys were drunk and went way too far. One thing's for sure, they need to learn to grow the [expletive] up."

That's a common theme among Griffin*Con regulars who feel betrayed by convention security for not removing these intruders from the crowd sooner. As charges are filed and litigation moves forward, check back to *Titan* for updates as they happen.

Part 3: The Hero's Journey

I

Saying that my sleep was troubled would have been an understatement. I wasn't so disconcerted by my dreams for their surreality, which was normally the case, but because of how much they echoed reality. I dreamt of a moment in my life I'd all but forgotten and it was puzzling to me that my subconscious would bring it back to me on this of all nights.

I was transported to a time and place from my youth. I was perhaps eight or nine years old, though I could see myself in my own adult body, merely in a child's size. In dreams it's always bizarre to recognize that you're in a dream and know that things are out of place but seem so ordinary that you do nothing about it.

Crawling over the top of the jungle gym, I knew exactly what was going to happen and I wanted to stop it. Unfortunately,

Bryan Young

I knew this to be a fixed and singular moment in time that was unchanging. Some of the small details might change in my subconscious telling of the story, but it had happened and would always happen for all recorded time and history.

Across the jungle gym was another little boy, about my age and happy. He looked nice enough and we'd been playing tag around the structure. The rules were you couldn't touch the ground or you were dead, adding a mortal consequence to the game.

I always marveled at how quickly kids could make friends. At that age, it's before you've put all of your barriers in place and can just sit in a room with someone and be fast friends for no better reason than being there.

Thinking back on the scene, I didn't see my mother, but the golden, setting sun was in my eyes, so she could have been anywhere. My playmate's mom lingered closer to us, easily within earshot. Her tense body language gave me the impression that, even for her nine-year-old, she was overprotective. She was that mom who would blow on his hot chocolate and make sure to tuck him into bed every night "snug as a bug in a rug" and give him a kiss and then stare at him like a loving serial killer until he was gently snoring.

We laughed and played and had a great time, but the boy was tiring and I was evading his every chance to tag me. Having never been terribly athletic, I was surprised that I was able to keep my frame agile enough to avoid the boy, whose name I never learned.

Sitting there, propping himself up on the metal tubes of the gym and catching his breath, he grinned a wide smile.

Not content to let him rest too long, I teased him to catch me. The first words out of my mouth were words I'd never said before and would never say again. I'd read this horrible word in a book and had no idea what it meant. In the book, it wasn't used in a context that would have implied how horrible and dirty a word it was; it seemed a good-natured insult.

And so with a playful bluster, I called out to him, "Come and get me, cunt face!"

My brain cued the sound of a scratching needle and everything stopped. The appalled and disgusted look on the mother's face was forever etched into my mind. Her jaw slackened, her eyes widened, her eyebrows raised, and her hand covered her mouth in shock. "What did you just say?"

My heart sank. Had I really done something wrong? Could words really hurt and cause such a visceral reaction? Would this poor woman tell my mother? That was my first concern. Quick on my feet, I tried reneging on my statement, "What do you think I said? I said, 'Come and get me *gun* face.' I said gun face."

But the offense this boy's mother suffered was too great and she pulled him off of the steel dome and marched him off of the playground. Once they reached the boundary of the park, they blurred out of focus and were smudged out of existence by what felt in my gut like the force of her anger alone. When they disappeared, they were followed by each piece of playground equipment. The slide vanished into black, then the swing set. After that the rocket shaped fort left me, then the jungle gym, too.

I was alone in an empty sand pit as far as the eye could see, feeling so utterly stupid, wondering how something so simple as a word could cut both ways so quickly. Clearly, it was offensive to that poor woman, and her reaction made me feel like I was a worthless piece of shit.

My child-sized adult dream avatar knelt down and began to sob.

I hated this moment in my life and I was sad and hurt that I had to live through it again. I'd worked so hard to forget it and I effectively did. My subconscious had betrayed me and showed my first truly agonizing moment of weakness.

The rest of my time in the dream was spent running in different directions trying hard to escape. Every scream I tried to let out was muted in that way that can only happens in nightmares.

I had no recollection of the moment my sleeping dreams turned to wakeful ones. It seemed like a faded line that passed from one to the other. I could tell when all the soreness and pain from taking so savage a beating came back to me. I didn't want to open my eyes and have the sleep I needed so badly escape me. Trying desperately to hold on to it, I spent the next while trying nod off. I tried counting each individual spot of pain on my body. I isolated each spot of pain, counted it, and checked it off a mental list, keeping my brain occupied just long enough for it to shut down again and bring me back to my dream state.

I was being chased by an axe murderer. Then I was counting spots of pain again. Then I was the axe murderer doing the chasing. Then I was quantifying the pain.

It was a miserable cycle that left me breathless and sweating. Sick of it all and wanting to break that cycle I finally got up out of bed.

Sylvester was on the floor, snoring like a champ. I supposed that one would sleep more soundly under a roof and a blanket if they were no longer accustomed to it.

Tiptoeing over him, I quietly locked myself in the bathroom, stripped down to my skin, and turned the shower on until the bathroom was steamed over and it wasn't possible to see myself in the mirror. Unlike the sweat from the fight yesterday, full of alcohol and adrenaline, I was misting in a clean, pure sweat. It felt good, but not as good as the stream of searing hot water rolling over my head and down my back.

My mind kept coming back to the dream and the dread it caused in me. I couldn't begin to imagine what that entire incident did to my psyche at such a young age. And what was my psyche trying to tell me by bringing it back?

I didn't like being confused. I was also sober and I didn't like that, either, but somehow it felt right. Suspicion instantly arose in my being. If this whole trip turned into a temperance message I was going to be fucking pissed. I could handle many things, but temperance was not one of them, for better or for worse.

Each drop of steaming water cleaned off the tiniest bit of the hurt, carrying it down off of my body and into the drain. As the water swirled down into the pipes, I braced myself, expecting at any moment that Marion Crane's blood would be circling with it. But that would imply that there's a killer in the bathroom and I'm not a killer. Maybe I'm Marion Crane. Maybe you don't even know what the fuck I'm talking about. Maybe no one does.

Jesus Christ.

Bryan Young

My hands were pruned and the water had lost its heated bite. I'd clearly overstayed my welcome. That was my style though.

Lost in thought about the previous night, I dried myself off and wrapped the towel around my waist. Wiping a thick, clear streak through the steam on the mirror, I took a long, hard look at myself.

It felt as though I was looking at myself for the first time. My face was older than I remembered it. Crows feet had sprouted around my eyes, punctuating four days of uneven stubble. Thick lines sunk into my cheeks around my mouth and my lips seemed thin. My hair was a coarse salt and mostly pepper when I distinctly remembered it being a nice, thick black.

My eyes were sunken in from too much booze and too little sleep and not in a way that could be fixed with taking a day off from drink and getting plenty of rest. It was a systemic problem that appeared gradually over the years and was, most likely, unable to be corrected.

That was okay with me.

I'd come to terms with the toll my actions would take on my body, but I'd never agreed to the toll time would take.

My body was wiry, thin, and doughy. There was no definition to it whatsoever. I was a puny runt covered in wisps of hair. Black and blue splotches of skin were spattered across my torso. Some bruises were uglier, a sickly green and yellow. There was little I could do for my soreness and less I could do for the marks of age that had become so apparent. So I did what I could: I rinsed my mouth out with a spearmint mouthwash and pulled my pants on one leg at a time, just like everyone else.

Quiet as a mouse, I collected my bag full of notebooks and writing utensils along with my laptop and I snuck out of the room, leaving Sylvester to sleep peacefully.

That mother-fucker certainly earned it after all I put him through the night previous.

The mass of people in the hotel lobby had thinned considerably since the night previous. Last night there was barely room to maneuver and breathe; this early morning there was room to walk in between people like I'd not seen since I arrived. Saturday night must have been the high water mark, the climax of the show, and certainly the climax of my time here.

Sundays were always like this wherever you went, with things feeling deserted. It was understandable here, too, what with it being the last day of the con. I imagine plenty of people were leaving early, others taking the time to stay an extra night so they didn't have to check out of their rooms.

Here we were on the last day and I was having a hard time deciding whether or not I wanted to leave. Nothing back home was calling to me. I couldn't get Laurie to call me back, my editor was still a wheezy fucking dirt bag, my job still sucked, and I was no closer to doing any sort of creative work than I'd been in the last year.

I was miserable and all of those people frolicking around me were having such a damned fine time without a care in the world. I couldn't tell if the majority around the hotel lobby were holdovers still partying from the night before, or if this was the morning shift that had gone to bed early so they could get there early enough to carry the party forward.

Bryan Young

Since the congestion was much less than ever, finding a portal out toward the rest of the offerings of Griffin*Con was no great trick. It would be easier to find something of interest since there was nothing in particular I wanted to do or see. I'd collected my most interesting stories across this weekend just meandering, so I supposed I'd just meander. I still just wanted to crawl up in a ball in the hotel room, but I had to get at least one more story.

As I traipsed through the hallways, I wondered all the while if there was any way I could milk another story out of the brawl. Maybe if I ran into the girl that was assaulted I could get her take on the whole thing. That would be worth another story, but anything short of that and I'd just be beating a dead horse with a stick.

I was the wrong person to send to this event, no question. My editor was just fucking with me and it disgusted me to think so. I wondered what I was missing in the world of politics right now. I'd been living in a cave this past weekend covering this convention and the President could have been assassinated for all I knew.

When I decided I didn't want to walk anymore because I was too achy and sore from my wounds, I popped my head into a random door. I had no frame of reference for where I was in the grand scheme of things. I couldn't point to where I was on a map of the convention, I simply didn't know. I'd traveled up and down escalators, up this way, down that way. If it weren't for the guy standing guard in armour with a Griffin*Con badge tied to his waist, I wouldn't have even been sure I was even still at the convention.

Attendance for this panel was low. There were perhaps twenty people scattered across a room designed for a hundred, each of them paying close attention to the trio of speakers on the dais, all taking furious notes. They were hanging on each and every word.

Taking a seat in the back was a pleasure on my legs and aching spinal column. Rifling through my bag, I withdrew a notepad and a pen. It was always easier for me to clear my head of thoughts if I could get them down through my arm and wrist and into ink. That, and people would lock me the fuck up if they caught me talking to myself. So, yeah. Two birds with one stone.

As soon as the pen hit the paper, ink flowed out directly from my brain. It was something I'd done since high school. I could just sit and put my thoughts down, and I'd put down any-thing my mind brought up. Sometimes story ideas would come out, stories for whatever rag I'd be working for or fiction stories. I'd written quite a bit of science fiction in years past. Very Twi-light Zone like. Not like most of the stuff at a place like this. Sometimes questions to myself would come out on paper. Some-times the only thing that would come was gibberish and doodles. But whatever came out there was a direct link from my heart to my brain to my hand and it was exactly that kind of soul searching I needed to be doing at the moment.

Some time had passed before I looked up and really *looked* at the speakers for the first time. They were each about guys my age, perhaps a little older. Two of them were sporting graying Vandykes and the third had a grizzly white beard. Each of the placards in front of them identified them as authors of some kind. Who knows what science fiction mumbo-jumbo they wrote for money, but there they were, paid for writing in a way that was decidedly more rewarding than the writing I was paid to do. They were living the dream, even if the literary elite would probably consider the content they produced trash. If the content these guys produced was considered trash, the science fiction I used to spend my time writing could easily be classified as fecal material.

They were talking about characterization and the structure of their novels; clearly those in the audience were aspiring novelists. Maybe fate and my aching body had brought me to exactly the right room in this entire convention.

The one in the graying beard and obnoxiously loud Hawaiian shirt was in the middle of a sentence, "...but that's what makes the most interesting characters, in my experience, is to put them through the ringer."

The one next to him concurred. He was a bit younger and wore a much more sensible shirt below a mop of wavy brown hair. "I think that's really at the key of it. The character, for him to be interesting, really has to go on that 'hero's journey.' He has to take that call to adventure whether he wants to go or not and he needs to go through so many trials he'll want to throw in the towel. And maybe he does throw in the towel, but he gets to the lowest point of his life, sometimes quite literally the bottom of a pit like one of the main characters in my last book, but he has to over come what's inside himself and then overcome the external. And once he's faced the worst he can inside the belly of the beast, he transforms into something new, a hero. And then he atones for what wrongs he may have committed in his past life and goes back to it, which is the hardest part. It's incredibly difficult to

take the lessons learned as a hero and ply them in life after return."

The third one, with the shortest hair and a turtleneck
stepped in at this point. "I'm sure a lot of you are familiar with
Campbell's monomyth? That's really all we're talking about here."

A hand shot up from the audience and was quickly called
upon to ask his question. "So, if you're writing all of these li-
censed characters from movies and the whole point of the movie
is them going on this quest, how difficult is it for you to expand
on that? I mean, if they've already gone on that hero's journey,
what is there left for you to write about?"

The middle one jumped in to respond first, "That's a
really interesting question, but the beauty of the monomyth is that
it's applicable to pretty much everything. Even you. That's what's
so great about it. The point of the hero's journey is to not be
afraid of fulfilling your dreams and slaying all of the beasts in the
way and, beyond all reason, overcoming. And these things can be
large or small. In the movies, obviously the characters go through
their more life changing arcs, true, but we still have to provide
more subtle character changes in their further adventures. It
makes tons of sense. Think about Luke Skywalker. There's not
much we can do to send him on a hero's journey more than what
happened in the films. And he could fall no further than learning
that the most hated villain and mass murderer in the galaxy had
not only just cut his hand off but turns out to be his father. And
what better arc could he take than from uninitiated farm boy to
Jedi Knight who overthrew the Empire? But if I were going to
write a book set after that, there are plenty of things he'd have to
overcome and defeat, both internally and externally."

Another picked up where the last left off, "See, for instance, he's going to train the next generation of Jedi Knights. Does he feel capable? Is it a responsibility or calling he wants? There are infinite obstacles that can be placed in his way that he has to overcome and when he comes out of it, he's a changed man and rewarded for it."

The third finished for them, "See, the stuff I write is based on a role-playing game, so I don't have that problem in any meaningful sense, but these guys are right. It's so easily applicable to your own life. You can't slay the demons in the physical world if you don't have the strength to slay the demons deep inside you. You have to unlock that potential in yourself before you can unleash it on the world. And as silly as it sounds, it was reading all of Campbell's work that got me from my day job to novelist. I had that dream inside me and I wouldn't lead a happy life if I didn't do it, no matter the cost. It was a mental block inside me that thought I couldn't make a living doing it. But that didn't matter. I could make all the money in the world but I'd still be miserable working a nine to five. That's the hero's journey. That's what it's all about. And if we can instill that into the myths of these books and the readers can decode that and apply that to their lives, then maybe we can smuggle something socially redeeming into our books, too. Right guys?"

They all agreed, nodding and bobbing their heads about.

Another hand shot up in the air, another question was asked and they answered. Things seemed muted for me. I was still soaking in all the information I'd just been given. It was good advice, sure. More importantly, it was exactly what I needed to hear. But I don't believe in fate and I don't believe in coincidence. I had to admit that at the most this was goddamned eerie. And this should have all been common sense, making me feel like a complete and total dotard. This was something I should have realized a long time ago.

Only a fucking idiot would need to be told so blatantly.

I was losing myself.

Not like I was losing myself by going crazy, I was losing myself in thought again. I had to keep writing until my quill runneth dry...or however that old trope went. This may have been the most interesting panel at this convention but I had this nagging desire to put something down. Something permanent. That's my favorite thing about ink, that's why I always write in pen, it's permanent. A thought that comes out from the heart in ink is indelible and somehow pure, much more pure than the erasable graphite of a pencil or the endlessly revisable clay of a computer's word processor. Inked pen was the paintbrush of a literary artist.

Jesus Christ, would you look at how pretentious I sound?

This panel dissipated and slowly faded into another as a brand new group of panelists and convention goers shuffled into the room, but I couldn't be bothered with any of it. I was filling page after page in my notebook, packing it margin to margin full of things I wanted to accomplish, questions about myself, why I was the way I was, and stories I wanted to tell.

It was slowly becoming a blueprint for the life I was too scared to lead.

The only reason I stopped was to sate the pangs of thirst and hunger that struck me. And I knew in my fragile physical condition if I didn't eat I'd never heal. And in my fragile emotional state I'd need a drink to calm my nerves and help me find my way.

And as lost as I was, I'd need all the help I could get.

There was a creak in my knees and a sharp pain in my back as I stood up, slowly like an old man. I inched toward the door and made it back outside.

The hallway was largely empty except for a faceless fellow in a skintight green leotard with a backpack talking to a knife-wielding girl dressed vaguely as Lewis Carroll's Alice. As much as I felt I finally understood some piece of why these people behaved as they did, I would never truly understand these people. But I didn't have to. What they did made them happy. And at the end of the day, isn't that reason enough?

Though I was fixated on Alice's skirt and the perfect legs beneath it that were covered sensually with white thigh-highs, I didn't notice that I'd run directly into a person. Maybe there *was* more going on in the hallway that I just didn't notice because I had an odd sexual overload for anyone dressed up as Alice in Wonderland. Which is a little weird since wasn't she like twelve in the books? This girl was not twelve, she was decidedly a woman.

But anyway, I'd run into someone and completely bowled them over. "Shit. I'm sorry... That was totally careless of me."

"No, you're okay, I was just~Hey!" Her voice changed as she looked up and realized who she was talking to.

My brain was elsewhere otherwise I would have recognized the girl instantly. It was Carrie or Katie or Susan or Jessica or... I didn't remember her name, exactly, but it was one half of the adorable duo that forced drugs upon me and showed me a good time until the night descended into madness. Sober, she still seemed incredibly attractive and smelled of an intoxicating vanilla lotion.

"Cobb." She smiled when she said my name. It was a warm and beautiful smile and it disarmed me completely.

"Yeah..."

"Katie. It's Katie."

"Right. How's things?"

"Things are great. I think this might have been my favorite Griffin*Con ever."

"I bet you say that every year."

"No. I really mean it."

"What makes you say so?"

She inched closer and got up on her tiptoes.

"Well, I've just sort of done what I wanted. Even the stupid crazy stuff. And it's been amazing."

Her fingers pulled me closer and before I knew what was happening, she pressed her soft, sweet lips against mine, kissing me sensually.

That feeling on my lips, that fire in my bosom, that could only mean I was day dreaming. Kisses didn't feel that incredible in real life, at least no kiss I've ever had. It truly was the kiss of my dreams.

The weight of her full, pouty lips seemed to have taken all of my worries and stress and set them aside.

Jesus. I needed more of that.

I snapped out of it and opened my eyes.

Jesus.

Bryan Young

It was no dream. Her deep brown eyes locked with mine and she pulled away, ending the kiss with a flick of her tongue against mine.

"Jesus."

She giggled coyly.

"What was that for?"

"We saw what happened last night. On G*CTV. And we heard why you did it. You're a real hero."

"You're delusional."

She laughed again, covering her mouth with an open palm.

God, she was cute. "Seriously. You're fucking crazy."

"You're a nice guy. You just need to let yourself believe it."

"That's no reason to kiss me."

"My goal this weekend was to kiss a nice guy. I haven't seen any others around."

"Surely you could have found an actual nice guy."

"You're the only one who made me laugh."

I found that hard to believe and said so.

She suppressed a laugh. "It was good seeing you around, Cobb. I'll be reading your stuff. If it's got your name on it, I'll be reading it."

She gave me a hug, pecked me on the cheek, and kept walking, heading in the opposite direction as me. I watched her walk away, paying careful attention to the sway of her delicate weight on her hips.

My god, she was beautiful.

After wiping the drool from my chin, I snapped myself out of an enamored state and back into my stupor. Katie's encouraging words and cleansing kiss didn't absolve me of my journey back into the hell I called home.

In fact, the more I thought about home, the more Katie's all too kind advance made things worse. It flooded back all of my suppressed memories of that first, magical kiss with Laurie. I'd tried to dam up all of my love for her with ambivalence, knowing that it was a river too great for me in this state. And the reminder of wading in those waters, that taste given to me by Katie, cracked the dam open. It didn't just crack it open, though, it exploded the dam into a thousand pieces in way that would bring a smile to the face of George Hayduke.

And all of that raging water came pouring into my heart, overwhelming it, drowning it.

Fuck me.

The food at the restaurant was tasteless and the beer offered no comfort. When your mind was elsewhere, it was hard to focus on flights of corporeal fancy like taste. Doubly so when your heart was barely treading water and ready to fill your lungs with metaphorical fluid.

Before I left to pack my things I decided to stop in at the dealer room and pick up a souvenir of some sort. Maybe I'd pick up something for Laurie. I was getting better: I only had to ask for directions once.

Something about the dealer room at this late hour made me feel as though I were roaming a street market in French Morocco during the war. All of the dealers were looking to unload as much merchandise as possible as quickly as possible. Shipping it home was cost prohibitive so they were all ready to make a deal.

Meandering through the aisles, I wondered what it was I'd fancy to bring home from this weekend. More importantly, what could I bring Laurie that would somehow be special and show her how much she meant to me? Aisle after aisle, row after row, nothing really caught my eye. Shopping for me was going to be easy. I think I needed something that was illustrative of my embracing of geekdom and decided on a shirt with a logo I *did* recognize on it.

Since he was my favorite during my formative years, I picked out a T-shirt for myself with a Batman logo across the chest.

For Laurie, I found a vendor that sold vintage posters and lobby cards for films of all sorts. As long as I'd known her, the closest thing Laurie had come to liking science fiction films was *The Wizard of Oz*. It was her favorite film, and when I came across a framed original lobby card, I thought it would be a nice gesture.

When I found out a framed original lobby card was thousands of dollars, I settled for the same thing, but as a much more affordable reproduction from 1955.

It still set me back a bit, but if it would get my foot back in the door with her then it would be worth it.

With no problems, I found my way back upstairs to my room, plunder in hand. It figures that the moment I've acclimated to the geography of this place is the moment I'm heading to my room to collect the last of my things and check out.

The plastic key hit the card reader lock, the light switched from orange to green and I entered my room for the last time.

To say that it was a disaster area would be a mild understatement. Sylvester had disappeared and in his wake only the comforter and pillow he'd used as a bed remained. The furniture I'd upended to barricade the door just two days ago was still strewn everywhere. There were bottles everywhere, empty pint glasses were scattered haphazardly, and all kinds of miscellaneous debris littered the ground. All of the courtesy snacks and bottles from the mini-fridge were shattered on the dresser. My clothes were hanging from every bit of furniture they could find purchase.

Piece by piece I stuffed my clothes into my bag, spending the better part of an hour collecting my things.

It shouldn't have taken that long to pack up. Maybe I was purposely stalling.

I closed the door to the room for last time, taking the "Do Not Disturb" sign from the knob and tossing it in a nearby garbage can. I'd have paid good money to see the face of the maid who had to reorganize that fucking pigsty.

Boarding the elevator, I could barely fit inside. There were four guys, each shouldering backpacks and hefting immense Tupperware tubs full of god knows what. They were dressed in street clothes, but were all still wearing Griffin*Con badges. They were the most normal looking humans I'd seen since I arrived at this overgrown costume party.

Remembering that I still needed at least one more story, I figured that maybe I could get some exit interview type quotes out of them. "You guys have a good time this weekend?"

"Of course."

"For sure."

"The best."

Bryan Young

"What was the highlight for you? Coming to this thing, I mean? Was it worth the money?"

"Griffin*Con is always worth the money, man. We trooped all weekend, had a badass time. Met up with old friends, met some idols. What more could you ask?"

I didn't know what I could ask, but I came up with one more burning question anyway: "What's in the Tupperware?"

They all said the word "armour" in unison and then the elevator dinged and we were all heading our separate ways via the hotel lobby.

I walked around the bank of elevators until I was able to determine which direction the front desk was in and then I dutifully got in line to check out. Half of me wanted to just bolt, burning the hotel and hopefully my employer. Did one even need to check out of hotels anymore? I wasn't sure, but I knew I didn't want to leave yet so I didn't mind waiting in line for a while longer. Sure, my plane was leaving tonight at the same time one way or the other, but being ass-raped by security at the airport for no good reason was just as bad as anything I'd go through at home. May as well put it all off as long as possible.

With a deep, cleansing breath, I took my place at the back of the line and waited.

"...honey, it was amazing. Just shush now. Shush. I need to make this call..."

The feeling I felt was that of utter disgust and I could feel the blood rush from my face. I knew that voice. I knew it and I wanted to smash it with a fucking pipe wrench.

"...oh! Hello? Yes, honey, this is Kira Castle from the best little movie show in the South?"

Fuck me.

There's only one thing that would be harder to stomach than having to stand listening to another conversation of Kira Castle's, but having to listen to only Kira Castle's half of that conversation while she shouted breathlessly, obliviously into a phone.

"Yeah, uh-huh! It was great to meet you at this little Griffin*Con thing, too."

She snickered and giggled at a joke that was never made.

"I was wonderin' if maybe we could get Alan to come in and do the show in the studio before he heads out of town."

My stomach heaved. I never wanted to throw up more in my life. This line wasn't moving fast enough and my stomach wasn't producing enough bile for me to puke on Kira Castle once more. A repeat performance of the other night would have been too good to be true.

"Well, I thought he said he'd be in town for a day or two. And the studio's just right near where he said he'd be stayin'."

What had I done? Of all the people to get in line behind me why did it have to be her? I might have been able to stomach anyone on this Earth, but not her.

"Well, yeah. Uh-huh. Nuh-uh, sugar."

She was getting louder into the phone.

"No. The studio's at my house. He can come right by. We can have tea and then we'll shoot in the studio."

This wasn't even getting more entertaining, just more painful.

"Uh. No. Yeah. It's the garage, honey."

I turned as though there was an imminent collision about to take place behind me and I caught her eye.

"Hello? Hello?" Apparently her tenuous contact had hung up. She put her phone back and without a hint of shame, her eyes met mine and they lit up.

"Oh, Mister...?"

"Cobb."

"Didn't I meet you the other day? I swear I've seen your face around here but it's been a very amazin' weekend."

Unbelievable.

I don't recall ever having vomited on someone, in spite or otherwise, and have them forget the incident entirely. Being vomited upon is a traumatic experience and I can't imagine it not being burned into the recesses of memory.

I smirked at her. "We did meet, I believe."

She offered her hand to shake and I took it with a limp grip. She wasn't even making eye contact with me as she shook, she was looking around for someone famous to cajole onto her show. That's when I realized why she didn't remember me. She was so self-absorbed that she didn't remember my face. It takes a special person to inwardly reflect something like that so she doesn't even notice who is doing the horrible thing to her, but to only focus on the damage being done to her personally.

Either that or my face was incredibly forgettable, which was entirely probably. In any case, she made me sick.

"It was the press party."

Her ears perked. Since I was press, clearly I might be able to be of some use to her.

"Oh, honey, I met so many people at that party and it ended so horribly... Remind me again?"

I popped the buttons on my shirt, revealing my brand new Batman T-shirt beneath.

"Guano."

And then she knew. The hamster in the wheel in her head was working double speed. She was barely intelligent enough to put two and two together. I was four, each one of the horsemen of the apocalypse, and for once in her life she had nothing to say for herself.

A slow smile crept across my face.

There were few things more satisfying than to watch over-confident people get into awkward situations that they wanted no part of and simply couldn't handle.

I wanted to laugh when she simply turned and walked away. There was nothing she could do or say and since I clearly had nothing to offer her but another vomit shellacking, further contact with me was pointless. And if I was going to vomit on her again, it was worth it for her to check out later.

Fucking bottom feeders.

It took me another fifteen minutes of standing in line, lost in my thoughts, before I was able to get to the desk and find out that all I needed to do was leave my key in my room.

Oh well.

The air outside was refreshing. I don't recall the last time I'd been outside. Cloistered inside the hotel for the convention I'd almost forgot what it was like to take in a cool fall breeze.

Dancing in front of the hotel was just the man I wanted to see. Sylvester was doing a dance on the sidewalk apropos of nothing, his enthusiasm being wafted into the air for all to absorb.

"You disappeared," I called out to him.

He stopped dancing and the smile on his face widened even further. "You first though, man. I figured I'd get while the gettin' was good. I didn't want to overstay your hospitality. Call me crazy, but you don't seem like a guy whose strong suit is kindness."

"You'd be right. It wasn't hospitality. It was business. You bailed my ass out. I'm a horrible photographer."

"And I saved your ass from gettin' beat."

"That you did."

"So you headin' back home now? Con's over, got nothin' left to stay for?"

"I just wanted to see you before I headed out. If you're ever up North, you should look me up. Maybe I could get you a job taking pictures."

"Me? No thanks. I see how much you hate what you do. I'd rather be happy and homeless than miserable workin' for shitheads."

"I wish I could say the same. I've grown too used to the comforts of shelter."

"Nothin' wrong with that."

I checked my wrist, pantomiming the action of reading a watch even though I didn't have one. "My flight is leaving soon. I need to get the fuck out of Dodge."

Sylvester walked me all the way back around the street and up the hill to the MARTA station. We chatted about the weekend, laughed about the brawl we'd been in, but overall the conversation was as light as the one we had when I came into the city.

As I was about to descend the monstrous escalator into the bowels of Atlanta, Sylvester grabbed me and embraced me in a deep masculine hug.

My bag fell to the pavement and my arms magically found their way around his solid frame. He beat the side of his fist three times against my back, solidly.

I was worried about the smell, but it wasn't so bad.

When Sylvester began talking into my ear in hushed tones it seemed somehow appropriate, not creepy at all. "You're a good man, man. That job you gave me, that's gonna help me out a lot."

"I'm a horrible person."

"More than the job though, man? You gave me back some respect. Ain't nobody who's done that for me in a long time."

He finally let go of me and we each took a breath and a step back.

"I didn't treat you with respect... I don't treat anybody with respect." I wanted to add, "Me, least of all," but I opted against it.

"Maybe you didn't. But you treated me the way you treated everybody else. And that don't happen to me. At all. I'm never gonna forget whatchoo've done for me, man. Don't ever think it don't mean a lot."

"Umm...thanks? I guess?

"You're welcome. Now get the fuck out of here or you'll miss your plane. I'm no good at goodbyes."

Were those tears in his eyes?

Jesus Christ.

Bryan Young

I put my hand on his shoulder, gripped it tightly in soli-
darity, and I took a deep breath as if to speak, "Take care of yourself, Sylvester."

And with that I descended into the Atlantean underworld
via moving staircase.

The train was waiting there with its doors open for me as
soon as I'd bought a ticket. They closed behind me instantly,
swallowing me inside the belly of the modern, sustainable convey-
ance.

Being in the train car was much the same as being in the
convention hall itself. I was surrounded by geeks with their luggage, all heading back to the airport. But this time they seemed to
grate on me less. They were more like real people. There was a
young couple, maybe not even old enough to drink, seated side by
side with their luggage stacked up in front of them. She wore a
bright red shirt with a girl on it with a speech bubble saying, "I
love you."

His shirt was a deep blue with a man on it, his speech
bubble said, "I know."

They were happy and content. This had been a good trip
for them. My mind raced through possibilities of why they could
be so happy, but it was then that I realized they had *every* reason to
be happy. There wasn't any single one. They were doing what
made them happy. It didn't matter if they looked like complete
fucking tools to anyone else, they were lost in themselves, in each
other. They whispered things to each other, eliciting giggles and
smiles from their opposite, and it was apparent that their entire
world consisted of nothing but the two of them. When they
looked in any direction, they looked right beyond it, as though

240

they were standing on a castle wall overlooking their magical kingdom of love and happiness. It would have been enough to make me sick if I didn't envy them so much.

And Jesus Christ did I envy them.

"I love you," she mouthed to him.

They were talking in the low tones native to lovers in public.

"Wasn't that great?"

"The best." Were they talking about the convention? Or sex? They could have been talking about anything.

"You want to come again next year?"

"I better."

"You will."

Trying to avoid an emotional overload, I gazed out the picture windows of the train and watched Atlanta shrink in size, smaller and smaller, until we entered the black tunnel the tracks led us to.

My heart trembled as I watched the young lovers disembark the train. They held each other's hands between them and with their outer hands pulled their luggage to the ticketing counter at the airport.

"Get a room, why dontcha," I muttered under my breath, realizing fully that they had just spent an entire weekend in a room, most likely fornicating in costume, almost certainly deep in love.

Before long I found myself waiting for my flight to board. The line for my boarding pass wasn't too bad and I was anally raped through security with a minimum of discomfort. It wasn't as demeaning than what the LSU fans put that girl through.

Lousy fucking bastards.

Sitting there. Waiting for the plane. The only thing I could think about was how much I wish I could turn things around. But I was a slave.

I was a slave to a paycheck. I was a slave to my filthy little editor. I was a slave to the corporeal needs of life as opposed to what would be fulfilling.

And I fucking hated it.

If only I had the courage to resign. I'd signed a contract, a commitment. But that bargain was clearly Faustian in nature.

But wasn't that my fault?

I knew it was Faustian to begin with. There was no surprise. The devil is in the details and I knew the fine print said I'd be miserable going in.

Why was it suddenly catching up to me?

I know I'd never have the courage to submit it, but maybe I should at least just write out a resignation letter. It could make me feel better if nothing else.

Right then and there, I resolved to write my hypothetical resignation letter. It would say everything I couldn't say to my editor's face.

It would be a manifesto that I could quietly and privately pull out each time things got too rough. And I could spend my nights fantasizing about actually turning it in.

"We are pleased to announce that we are now boarding flight eight-fifteen with service to Ronald Reagan National Airport at gate A23."

Reagan. Fucking Reagan.

Before I boarded, I pulled out my notebook and I would shut out all things to write my manifesto. I only wish I had the guts to actually submit it.

This was me at my lowest.

AUTHOR GROWS A SPINE
or COBB'S RESIGNATION
By M. Cobb

By now you must know how much I hate my
job. I hate the way it makes me feel. I
traded my integrity for a steady check and
the trade off wasn't worth it.

My life is worth much, much more than what
I've been put through, and your publication
(read: second rate webpage) is a travesty.
It is something unholy and degrades the
journalistic profession more than you can
ever imagine because you lack the vision
required to bring things to new heights.

You waste your writers on stories they
don't know or care about, you force us to
write about things that don't matter, you
make us talk down to our readers and give
them even less respect than they deserve,
and you play everything to the lowest common denominator.

At its best, journalism can raise the human
level of awareness to problems and cause
them to take action. At its worst, in the
case of *Titan*, it panders to an audience,
giving them insights to things they need to
know nothing about. It's not enlightening

to anyone. We are a content farm of information that no one needs, to build links
for advertisers who make products no one
wants. We are the scum of the journalism
world and you know it.

We do this for all the wrong reasons and
you rule over it with an evil, iron fist
and I've had enough of it.

We're not saving the world. On the contrary, I think our emphasis on triviality
and celebrity cheapens the world and damages it permanently.

You know full well that the world won't
stop turning if you treated us with the
modicum of respect those in our profession
deserve.

My resignation is effective immediately.
I'm going to take some time off and work on
my book, something that could very well
change the world. I've learned a lot of
things on this last assignment, and chief
among them is that there can be stories
told that show us the best of what we can
be.

It will make me happy. And then I can dedicate some time into finding a position as a political columnist where I'll be respected and my analysis will be read and used to influence the people of the United States into coming back from the brink of insanity.

I can and WILL make a difference.

Sincerely,

Michael Cobb

II

"What the fuck is this horse shit?" There was trouble in his voice.

"What does it look like?"

Instead of wearing sunglasses, I was staring at my former editor right in his beady, reptilian eyes. He hadn't gotten any less disgusting over the weekend. He had the complexion of a sweaty pizza and was nervous. I'd finally found a way to hurt him.

"It looks like you're sending me up shit creek."

He had my resignation letter in his hand and was waving it around. Each word he spat out of his mouth was accompanied with a spray of garlic infused saliva.

Somewhere in the middle of writing my resignation letter I'd gathered the resolve to submit it. No more would I cower beneath this man for table scraps. I was a journalist and a writer, goddamn it, and I would not be treated as anything less.

He was more than welcome to hire some dopey college intern to take over my position. Hell, that's the sort of person who would be grateful for such an opportunity. Snot nosed kids right out of college didn't know any better. But I did and I was done with it.

"Why are you going? You're the best writer I've got in my stable."

"Then maybe you should have started treating me like your best writer."

"I had to challenge you, wake you up outta your funk. You know how it is. I had to do something drastic. Get you outta your comfort zone."

"I wish I could believe that."

"You've got to."

I don't think he liked me staring at him. He preferred me to wear the sunglasses in his office, especially now that I had fire in my belly and daggers in my eyes. I was a fucking steamroller and he knew it was imperative to get the fuck out of my way.

He folded my resignation letter and dropped it on his desk, avoiding the intensity of my gaze. "Why don't we just forget about all a' this? I'll see what I can do about getting you a little bit of a raise."

I didn't flinch. My stare grew deeper. I was no longer looking at him but through him. I had heat vision and I was burning holes in his hubris.

"Tell you what. I'll even make you the politics editor for *Titan*. You'll never have to cover this Mickey Mouse bullshit again."

That fire in my belly rose into my chest and came out of my mouth with all the flame and fury it deserved. "Everything I said in my letter stands. You're a tiny fucking person running a shitty outlet and I want nothing to do with you."

"Hey, no need to get personal. I get it. You don't like me. But you've got every other reason in the world to stay on. But more than that, how're you going to survive long enough to write a fucking novel? And you said it was—what? Science fiction? That's just fucking ridiculous. Who do you think you're kidding?"

"No one, for once."

"That convention was a bad influence on you. And really, you know as well as anyone print is dead."

"I don't fucking care if print is dead. It's what's going to make me happy. And that's worth more to me than any raise or promotion you could give me. You don't get it and you never will. You get your kicks running people down and pulling the fucking strings, but I'm not a puppet. And I'm done with it. I'll find free-lance gigs to skate me by, but I am not standing for this anymore. At any price."

He was still talking, begging me to stay, when I went for the door. But before I left, I said to him, calmly and coolly, "Happiness is worth more than all the money in the world and after forty years, I'm finally on the path to find mine."

And with that, I was gone.

There was a box of my belongings on my desk that I collected on my way out, tucked underneath one arm. Some part of

Bryan Young

me wished I had more to offer on my way out than the middle finger, but arson was never really my style.

Maybe it had been my style before, but I didn't wish any of these fuckers any harm. I just wanted to get out of there. Forever.

Never again did I want to look up from my desk and out the window and see the cheap, painted brick of the building that went up nine inches next to us, obscuring our views of the building across the vacant lot. Never again did I want to hear that ugly cuss call me into his office for an assignment. Never again did I want to smell that mix of electronic ozone and feces that I'd been accustomed to. Never again did I want to walk down the lonely hallway of shame to the stairwell, and never again did I want to take the six flights of stairs down to the liberation of the street. And thanks to my new attitude, I'd never have to.

The cool air nipped at my face, invigorating my mind. All I could do was lose myself in thought. I was on a mission.

I don't know what it was specifically that changed my mind about handing in my resignation letter as soon as I got home, first thing Monday morning. It was no bullshit that I was still terrified about the uncertainty. What would happen if my novel didn't pan out and I couldn't put together enough freelance work to keep myself afloat?

It was a real worry. Acting courageous was one thing, but I didn't have the fortitude to live on the street like Sylvester. But I had a little bit socked away to get me by for a little while.

The thing that had slain the dragon inside me, though, was the prospect that I'd be doing something with my life that felt worthwhile. I hadn't felt that way in a long time. And if I felt worthwhile, maybe Laurie could find me worthwhile, too.

She wasn't home when I'd arrived the night previous. She was out all night. I could only guess that she knew I was coming back and simply wanted to avoid me.

I couldn't blame her. When I left I was a different person. I was simply an ambitionless drunk who existed merely to occupy space. Maybe I was still a drunk, but I had a goal now, ambition. And I had the wherewithal and courage to fight for her. We were going to be together like I needed to be or I was leaving. I didn't want to leave, but if I couldn't have her, I couldn't be her roommate. A clean slate is what I needed, with or without her.

Maybe I could have my cake and eat it, too. Maybe she'd see me as the new person that I was. Maybe she could love me again since I had hot irons in the fire, full of ambition and promise. Maybe that's what we'd been missing all these long years I'd been at *Titan*.

Maybe when I finished my novel, she'd come back to Griffin*Con with me. That seems like the perfect place to publicize my novel and sell it and I'd love to share a taste of my experience with her. I was one of them now and maybe she could be, too.

On the other hand, it could all backfire and she could hate me for the rest of my days regardless. Was it the sight of me that she'd grown to find so disgusting? That would be disheartening because it was the one thing I couldn't do a damn thing about.

But was that even possible?

She loved me once. At least it seemed to be love. Wasn't that proof positive that she was capable of loving the outer me? And if the inner me was so much more full of life and spirit, wouldn't that be an added selling point?

Normally I'd have taken the train home, but today I couldn't stop moving. I was a hummingbird beating my new wings. If I stopped moving, I'd fall right out of the sky.

Walking all the way home from my place of employ-ment—former place of employment—was something I'd never done. It never occurred to me. I was accustomed to doing things as quickly and easily as possible, but that was the old me. The new me does what feels right, even if it was harder.

As soon as I got home, I'd walk in that door and I'd lay it all out to Laurie. I needed her. I wanted her there by my side. I wanted her there next to me, falling asleep to the sound of my typewriter. I wanted to dote on her and treat her the way she deserved to be treated, not in the shitty manner that me and every other fucking guy she was mildly involved with was treating her. She wasn't going to be used up simply because she had a vagina and needs. She was going to be treated like a person of her intelligence deserved. I'm not just talking about opening doors for her, either. I wanted to give her everything I hadn't before. She was my equal in every way and I wanted her to be my partner. My co-pilot.

This was the best I could offer her, and if she refused it, sure it would be heartbreaking, but I'd understand. You can't just change your way of thinking and the way you want to be and the way you want to treat people overnight, tell them so, and expect them to believe you. I'm not an idiot, I knew it would take hard work, and she'd be a fucking retard to take my word for it. I'd have to show her. And I couldn't blame her if she didn't give me a chance but I'd be foolish not to try.

But I needed a commitment. No more guys coming over. If we were going to make this work, it was going to be just me.

My heart fluttered. I was there. There was nothing that would stop me. I knew I was a drunken mess, but at this moment I felt like Prince fucking Charming on my way to kiss Sleeping Beauty. If only I could convince her that I really was Prince Charming. No, that kind of thinking was defeatist. Fuck it. I *would* convince her. There was no other way.

I was going to follow my bliss and make it hers.

With one turn of the knob to our apartment I was going to change my world and everyone else's.

"Laurie, I'm home!"

"So what?" she shouted from the bedroom.

"We need to talk," I shouted back.

And boy, did I mean it.